THE SHADOW IN THE DARK

Attempting to escape the scandal that has engulfed her, Daisy Lewis leaves home and heads for the Cornish town of Pencarrow, still as beautiful as she remembers from her childhood holidays. But news spreads like wildfire in the small, tightly knit community, and soon she must deal with a blackmailer who recognises her from her previous life. Even worse, she suspects it could be one of the two handsome men who are keen to romance her. Is there anyone Daisy can trust — and will her secret be exposed yet again?

SUSAN UDY

THE SHADOW IN THE DARK

Complete and Unabridged

LINFORD
Leicester

First published in Great Britain

First Linford Edition
published 2016

A catalogue record for this book is available
from the British Library.

ISBN 978–1–4448–3021–7

Published by
F. A. Thorpe (Publishing)
Anstey, Leicestershire

Set by Words & Graphics Ltd.
Anstey, Leicestershire
Printed and bound in Great Britain by
T. J. International Ltd., Padstow, Cornwall

This book is printed on acid-free paper

1

Daisy Lewis pointed her Volkswagen Polo in the direction of the motorway and pressed her foot hard on the accelerator, her destination the small Cornish town of Pencarrow on the south coast. She, her brother, and her parents had spent several holidays there, and although Daisy had only been a child at the time, she had no trouble recalling every perfect moment of it. In a desperate attempt to recapture just a fraction of that happiness, a week ago she'd arranged to rent a cottage for the next six months. She thought she remembered it, in particular its exterior pastel-blue walls. She hoped they'd still be blue, and as it had retained the name Blue Haven, she guessed they would be. Her mother had laughingly told her many years later that she'd been so struck by those that at first she'd insisted on calling it Blue Heaven.

Daisy definitely remembered that it over-looked Sandy Cove, the small beach where she and her brother had spent so many hours with their endlessly patient parents. The parents who'd been aghast when she'd told them what she intended to do now.

Her father, Tom, had pleaded, 'Please don't leave. It'll all blow over eventually. These things always do. Just be patient. It's only been a couple of months.'

Eve, her mother, had then added her own heartfelt appeal. 'Listen to your dad, love. We can help you get back on your feet. You can stay here with us.'

'No,' Daisy had said. 'It's very kind of you both, but I have to go. I'm sorry, but I'm sick of being pointed at, whispered about, and shouted at.' *And getting bricks through my window and obscenities daubed on my door,* she'd silently added. Her parents didn't know about either of those incidents, mainly because her father would have reported both to the police, and that had been the last thing Daisy had wanted. She'd had enough adverse publicity to last her a lifetime and beyond, and that snippet of news would have been seized upon and promptly plastered all over the front pages of the national newspapers, along with her photograph. Again.

'I need to be able to hold my head up somewhere where no one will know me or what happened. I'm tired of creeping around, trying not to be noticed.'

Besides, Daisy knew that her parents' house was too small to comfortably accommodate her as well as them. They'd be living on top of each other; and her parents, as much as she knew they loved her, would swiftly tire of that. They'd assured her they wouldn't when she'd pointed it out, but she knew better. They'd grown accustomed to having their own space, as she had in her own home. A home that had been considerably larger than her parents', and with every conceivable luxury. That, however, had been repossessed by the bank when she'd told them she couldn't afford to carry on paying the mortgage on it.

She had managed to sell a lot of the furniture, which she hoped would provide her with sufficient funds to live on for a limited period, and the rest she'd donated to various charities. But once she was installed in the cottage, she knew she'd need to find some sort of job. The longest her money would last was three or four months, as a good portion of it would need to go on simply living day by day.

'I'll call you once I arrive,' Daisy assured her desperate-looking mother.

'Promise?' Eve said.

'I promise.'

'Okay, well, drive safely then.'

'Mum, stop worrying. At the age of thirty, I think I can look after myself.'

But despite her brave words, once she eventually reached the M5 heading south she found herself questioning whether she was indeed doing the right thing. She kept going, however, and the miles were quickly swallowed up, so it didn't feel all that long before she was crossing the Somerset border into Devon.

With the thought that she'd soon be in Cornwall, she felt her taut nerves begin to relax as memories flooded back of their holidays all those years ago. Of course, it wouldn't be the same now. For starters, she wouldn't be on holiday. She swallowed nervously. At least no one would recognise her, even if they'd read the newspaper reports and seen her photographs — or so she hoped. She stretched up and briefly glanced in the rear-view mirror at her own reflection instead of the road behind.

She barely recognised herself. Because of what she'd been forced to endure, she'd lost weight, so the bones of her face, mainly her cheekbones, were more prominent; her chin was sharper too. Even her figure had slimmed down from a size fourteen to a twelve. But the main difference was her hair. She'd had it cut short, very short, no more than a couple of inches all over and feathery, so that it framed her face in soft tendrils. She'd then changed the colour from its natural mahogany-brown to honey-streaked blonde. It had transformed her, making her eyes look twice their normal size and bluer, almost violet, in fact; and luminous. Or so she'd been assured by her best friend. Daisy didn't know quite what luminous meant in the context of the eyes. Illuminated? How the hell could eyes be illuminated?

Daisy's glance then went to the rear seat. It was packed with the few possessions she'd been unable to bring herself to part with. They were presents that had been given to her over the years by family and friends; things like her silver-backed hairbrush and mirror, a treasured gift from her now-deceased godmother, Alice. Her jewellery box was there, containing the few items she'd kept, mainly for sentimental reasons; the rest she'd sold. As she'd told herself, she'd hardly need expensive jewellery where she was going. The trouble was, she'd received just a fraction of their true value.

There was another large box of her favourite books, along with the photo albums that had belonged to her grandmother before she died. They provided almost a complete family history. There was a small antique clock that had also belonged to her grandmother, and which her mother had insisted she take with her, assuring Daisy that she herself had no use for it. Completing the list was a small mosaic-topped table, which her mother had again claimed she had no use for; her laptop; a radio; and a portable television. It was all there with her so she'd have some mementoes of home and family.

All of a sudden, the sign for Okehampton loomed up. Daisy turned the car and headed that way. Shouldn't be long now, she reckoned. She glanced at the clock on the dashboard. Three forty-five. With luck, she should be in Pencarrow by five fifteen. She'd go straight to the estate agent and pick up the key to the cottage before they closed for the day. She'd have time then to find Blue Haven, unpack the car, and settle herself in before it grew dark.

The late October days were shortening and the clocks would go back at the weekend, shortening them even further. Daisy wondered what winter would be like in this southern seaside town. Milder than what she was used to, she hoped.

But the remainder of the journey proved slower than she'd anticipated, as the traffic was surprisingly heavy, so it was just a minute or two short of five thirty by the time she arrived. She managed to find a convenient parking space on a nearby quay. She'd already passed the estate agent's as she'd driven along Fore Street; it was still open, so she ran straight to it.

'I thought you weren't going to make it before we closed for the day,' the smiling man standing inside told her.

'*I* thought I wasn't going to make it,' she riposted.

As she'd already settled the payment that was due for the cottage, all she had to do was collect the key and receive directions for how to find it.

'There's a folder with information on how everything works in a drawer in the kitchen dresser,' the agent told her. 'The bed in the main bedroom hasn't been made up, as you want to use your own linen, I believe. And you've also agreed to do your own cleaning, so — '

'Yes, that's right.' That way, she wouldn't be using up any more of her precious money than she had to.

'Okay. Well, that's all confirmed, so all I can say is have a good stay. Any complaints, bring them to me.'

Daisy smiled at the man. 'I will, thank you. I'm sure I'll see you around.'

It proved an easy task to locate the cottage, even though she had to continue on out of the town and then follow the main road back in again due to the one-way system that was in operation nowadays. This time, instead of driving down into Fore Street, she turned right and drove along a road she remembered from her holidays here, the Esplanade. It followed the curve of the estuary. She had forgotten how beautiful it was; the sun was setting and bathing the town in a golden glow, at the same time beaming a pathway across the water to the other side and the even smaller town of Polcurno.

Blue Haven, when she reached it, sat in total isolation at the bottom of a steep hill; its walls, as she'd expected, still pastel-blue. You couldn't take a car any further, which meant only walkers would have any reason to pass the cottage. Through the fast-gathering dusk, she glimpsed the rough track that led up directly to the headland above; and there, just as she remembered, was a ruined castle. She and her brother had only ventured up there on their own once. Their parents had discovered what they'd done and promptly forbidden them to go alone. She could see why now. One misstep and they'd have been over and onto the treacherous rocks below.

Daisy sat in the car and gazed around. Just beyond the headland, she could see the open sea. She drew a deep breath as her doubts about what she was doing resurfaced. It was a lonely spot, and without a single street light it would be totally dark once the sun had dipped beneath the horizon. Her misgivings deepened as she opened the car door and climbed out. She was being stupid, she firmly chided herself. Nonetheless, she couldn't help but glance around. But there was no one there; no one to taunt her, whisper about her, or frighten her with a brick through the window. She'd keep herself busy, she resolved, and that would drive away these disturbing thoughts. She'd open the front door and unload her belongings from the car. Then she'd prepare herself some food before unpacking it all. Everything was going to be okay. It was exactly what she'd wanted. No neighbours; not a single person to bother her.

Grabbing her jacket from the front passenger seat and slipping it on — the evening had developed an autumnal chill to it, she'd noticed on her way to the estate agent's — she strode to the door and fitted the key into the lock. It turned easily and the door swung open into a small hallway, where she was confronted by two closed doors. She opened the nearest one and found herself in a kitchen. It was compact, but a quick glance around showed that it contained all she'd need: a cooker, a fridge-freezer, a washing machine, and even a small microwave oven on the worktop. A tiny round table with two chairs sat in front of a window alongside a pretty dresser. The window looked out directly onto the road.

She returned to the hallway and opened the second door. It led into a surprisingly large, comfortably fur-nished sitting room with windows stretching the entire length of one wall; the other three were painted in a colour that reminded her of clotted cream. Appropriate, she decided with a smile. The carpet was pastel-green, and the three-seater settee and two armchairs were upholstered in a fabric the exact shade of a bowl of oatmeal.

There was a flat-screen television and a bookcase crammed with the sorts of books Daisy enjoyed reading. She spotted a couple by P.D. James, three by Kate Morton, an Erica James, and several by one of her favourite authors, Jodi Picoult, plus many more by other popular writers. She grinned to herself; plenty there to while away the long winter evenings. A low coffee table was positioned in front of the settee, and a medium-sized log-burner stood in a pretty stone fireplace, a small table placed either side of it upon which sat a couple of lamps. The log-burner was a particularly welcome sight; she'd definitely make use of that. She'd already noticed the pile of ready-cut logs neatly stacked against the wall of the cottage in a space that she assumed was for her car.

There were French doors fitted into the centre of the windows. She crossed the room and opened them with the key that was already in the lock, before stepping outside onto a paved terrace. She was looking down onto the beach that lay beyond a low brick wall: Sandy Cove. She raised her gaze and found herself staring directly out to sea.

The unpacking could wait. Despite the deepening dusk, she sat down on one of the four chairs that surrounded an oblong table and gazed around. She spotted a set of shallow stone steps to one side of the terrace that led down into a garden that was mainly lawn but had a couple of what looked like herbaceous borders. There were a few remaining plants still with flowers on. Two palm trees framed the view across the water. She saw that the lights were on all over Polcurno, reassuringly twinkling at her, and all of a sudden she didn't feel quite so alone. She imagined people in their homes preparing meals, watching television, reading the paper.

Eventually Daisy dragged her gaze away from all of this and looked upwards to the road she'd just driven down. There were more lights shining on this side of the harbour, and she could make out a house perched precariously, it looked to her, on the very edge of the cliff, just where the road began its descent to her cottage. She'd forgotten that it was there and hadn't noticed it from the road. She'd passed a row of thick bushes and trees, now she came to think about it. It must be behind those.

She gave a soft sigh and zipped up her jacket, at the same time tugging the collar further up her neck. With the setting of the sun a small breeze had arisen, its chill nipping at her ears. Never mind. She sighed contentedly. For all her initial doubts, she could be happy here. She'd have the space and the solitude, and more importantly the time to lick her still-festering wounds.

* * *

With her belongings unpacked from the car and placed where she wanted them, and the double bed made up in her cream-painted room, Daisy prepared herself a simple meal from the cold bag of food she'd brought with her. Afterwards she rang her parents on the landline — she hadn't been able to get a signal on her mobile phone — and reassured them of her safe arrival.

'You'll have to come and stay, Mum,' she said. 'It's gorgeous. There's a guest room; it's got a sea view. Both bedrooms have, in fact. It's wonderful. You'll love it.'

'Oh, love, it's such a relief to hear from you. Now, give me your landline number. I presume you have one?'

'Yes, that's what I'm phoning on; my mobile doesn't seem to work at the moment. I'll try again tomorrow.'

She ended the call and went to find the folder with details about the cottage and its facilities. She knew there was broadband available — she'd already found the router — and she wanted to connect her laptop ready to use the following day. With that done, she opened a bottle of wine and toasted her new home, at least for the next six months.

After that, well — who knew? She sat in an armchair facing out of of the huge window and watched what she guessed were the lights of two fishing boats leaving the harbour for a night's work.

Finally she went upstairs to the bedroom and slept, for the first time in weeks undisturbed by dreams and fears about what troubles the following day might bring. She awoke the next morning to the sound of the waves washing onto the beach and the shrill calls of the seagulls. She climbed from bed, also for the first time in weeks eager for the day ahead to begin. She swept the curtains back, opened the window wide, and leant out. A black cormorant flew low over the water, heading upriver; and as if to enhance the already idyllic scene, a couple of children ran around the sandy beach.

She took a deep breath of the ozone-laden air, filling her lungs to capacity. Marvellous. She looked upwards then. The sky was blue and the sun was beaming down, festooning the sea with a dressing of diamond studs. She glanced at the clock on the bedside table and saw that it was just after nine thirty. She smiled. She'd slept for over eleven hours.

Her mobile phone buzzed. Wow, even that was working. Could she ask for anything more? She grinned and picked it up. It was a text message from her friend, Sally. 'Hope all is okay. Call me or email me. Can't wait to hear from you.'

She yawned. She'd do it after breakfast. For now, she was in desperate need of a cup of strong coffee.

★   ★   ★

An hour later she was dressed and, tempted by the glorious morning, was quickly heading off in the direction of the town. A walk would do her good, she'd decided. Besides, after the long drive the day before, she needed the exercise. There were several other things she also needed, mainly food and fresh vegetables. She'd already been online and ordered a few gadgets for the kitchen, the chief item being a cafetiere.

It took twenty minutes of brisk walking to simply reach the end of the Esplanade, but she didn't mind. The morning had remained bright and surprisingly warm, so warm she'd taken off her jacket and tied it by the sleeves round her waist. And it was a stunningly pretty walk, with sea views practically all the way. On the other side of the road, the few trees that there were had leaves that had turned bronze and orange, the colours so vivid they shone. They were luminous, in fact, to quote Sally. Daisy grinned to herself. She was just about to turn into the town when the sight of several yachts zigzagging across the harbour in the morning breeze proved irresistible, and she stopped for several minutes to watch them before walking on.

Pencarrow, as she'd realised the afternoon before, had hardly changed in the twenty or so years since she'd last visited. It was every bit as picturesque and quaint as she remembered it. Most of the shops had changed ownership, obviously. One in particular drew her towards it. The window was full of the most exquisite glassware. There was everything from coasters to huge, extravagant bowls and dishes; there was even some jewellery, she noticed. She went inside and began to examine a couple of items that particularly interested her.

The woman who she assumed was the owner, judging by her proprietary air, watched her closely; rather too closely for comfort, in fact. Did she think Daisy was planning to steal something? 'Are you here on holiday?' she finally asked, her brown eyes gleaming with what belatedly looked to Daisy like simple curiosity.

'No,' Daisy said, 'I've rented a cottage for the winter. Blue Haven.'

'I'm deeply envious. It's lovely out there. On your own, are you?'

'Yes, I am.' She lowered her gaze once more to the bowl she'd been examining, hoping the other woman would take the hint and stop questioning her. Her tactic didn't work.

'Bit lonely for you, isn't it?'

Daisy looked back at her, resigning herself to telling the woman what she wanted to know. Were all the locals going to be this inquisitive? If so, she'd have to be very careful how she answered their questions. One careless reply and her cover could be blown. Even this far south, they must have read all about it. 'A bit, but I love it. The view's to die for. I used to holiday here with my parents and my brother twenty years or so ago.'

'Oh, so you remember your way around?'

'More or less. Do you live here?' She felt desperate to move the conversation away from herself.

'Yeah, I was born here.'

'Lucky you.'

'I did leave at one point. Itchy feet got the better of me. I ended up in Lancashire — Blackpool, of all places. Didn't stay long there. I moved back down to Southport instead. More my sort of place.'

'Oh, I — ' Daisy stopped speaking abruptly. 'I know it.' She smiled weakly, agonisingly aware of how close she'd come to maybe giving herself away. 'By the way, I'm Daisy; Daisy Lewis.'

'Hello, Daisy Lewis.' The woman held out a hand. 'I'm Freya Carne.' Her gaze then was a keen one. It was if somehow she'd sensed Daisy's momentary slip. The whole thing had brought home to Daisy how cautious she'd have to be. Not that it was likely anyone down here would recognise her. Still, best to play things safe, even if it did seem a touch paranoid.

'So where are you from?' Freya went on to ask.

Daisy thought quickly. 'Liverpool.'

'You don't have a Liverpool accent.'

'No, my mother made sure I didn't.'

Freya continued to regard her. Her stare was beginning to make Daisy uncomfortable. 'What made you decide to come down here for the winter?'

Daisy shrugged. 'I fancied a change. I-I've just come out of a difficult relationship and I needed to get away.' Which wasn't strictly a lie.

'Huh, I'd just like to be *in* a relationship,' Freya snorted. 'Hey, tell you what. I don't expect you know many people yet. A couple of friends and I are meeting for a drink this evening at the Ship pub. You probably passed it — ?' Daisy nodded. 'Why don't you come along, and I'll introduce you to them. You'll be very welcome. Several of the locals congregate there.' Her smile was a warm one and softened what had been till then a rather plain face, with narrow eyes and slightly-too-large nose and wide mouth. The mousy hair, styled in an unflatteringly straight bob, had simply exaggerated the impression of plainness. Her clothes didn't do much for her either: a well-worn and much-laundered cream jumper, which she'd teamed with a pair of skinny jeans. All the outfit did was emphasize a figure that was far too thin; angular, even.

Daisy hesitated, her confidence in her changed appearance and its capacity to deceive people vanishing in an instant. They all must read the newspapers, even in this remote part of the country; and as her father had unthinkingly pointed out, it was only a couple of months since everything had blown up around her. If anyone recognised her, her plans for a future here would be in tatters. Her heart began to hammer in her chest. 'Oh — well, I don't . . . '

'Oh, come on. We're all pretty harmless. We've even stopped wrecking ships.' Daisy stared at her. Freya was grinning — at her own joke? At least, Daisy presumed it was a joke. Whatever, the other woman was making the invitation hard to resist.

And she was being rather stupid, Daisy told herself; overly sensitive. She had to get out and meet people. She couldn't turn into some sort of reclusive hermit. In which case, she might as well get the whole business over with sooner rather than later. Then no one would begin to wonder why she was keeping herself to herself, and start asking difficult questions.

'Okay, then. Thanks. What time?'

'Eight o'clock. See you there.'

Eventually Daisy left the shop, but not before she'd purchased a beautiful glass bowl and a set of four coasters. She felt a stab of guilt. They hadn't been cheap and she really needed to curtail her spending, at least until she knew how much money she'd need for her day-to-day expenses. But oh, what the hell. She'd look upon it as a house-warming present to herself, from herself. And the bowl would look wonderful on her mosaic table in the sitting room. The combination of the jewel-like colours would brighten the plainly decorated room.

She grinned, glancing down at the bag she was carrying — which was why she failed to notice the three people standing at the edge of the pavement immediately in front of the shop door as they waited to cross the road. As a result, she walked straight into them and only just managed to save her bag with its precious contents from slipping out of her grasp and crashing on the ground.

2

'Hey, steady on.'

The man she'd so heedlessly walked into swivelled round and grabbed her by the shoulders, only his sheer strength and dexterity stopping them both from staggering into the road and the path of a car. For her part, Daisy dragged the carrier bag up to hold it protectively between the two of them.

'Oh, uh — s-sorry,' she gasped. 'I wasn't looking.'

'That's obvious,' the stranger irritably went on. He frowned as he released her from his grasp. 'Do you usually walk around not looking where you're going? Must make for some interesting expeditions. Tell me, what was the last thing — or person — you crashed into?'

Her own irritation mounted at this uncalled-for display of irony; after all, she hadn't deliberately walked into him.

27

She looked up and found herself staring into a pair of heavy-lidded slate-grey eyes. Her gaze then took in the dark blond hair, a strand of which had fallen onto his forehead. The nose was pure Grecian. He had chiselled cheekbones, a perfectly shaped mouth, and a firm jawline. Here, she conceded, was someone to be reckoned with. Not least because he must be at least six feet one or two. He certainly towered above her five feet five inches. He also had the sort of build, plainly visible beneath the sweater and jeans he was wearing, that suggested he took regular and strenuous exercise.

'Lex Harper,' he went on before she could offer any sort of response to his sarcasm, 'and my daughters Chloe and Imogen.' He pointed to the girls standing alongside him, one after the other, as he said their names.

Daisy didn't much care for the expression in Chloe's eyes. What was it? Suspicion? Not of her, surely; she'd only just arrived in the town. Or could it be that she actually did think Daisy had bumped into her father deliberately? If that was the case, the girl didn't put the accusation into words. Instead, she muttered, 'Oh God, not another one. Will they never stop?'

Which, upon reflection, did seem to confirm Daisy's suspicion that the girl thought she'd walked into her father deliberately. But for what reason? To force him to notice her? From the sound of it, women did so on a regular basis.

'Say hello, girls,' Lex commanded.

Daisy wondered if he'd heard what his daughter had said. If he had, why hadn't he admonished her? The remarks had obviously been aimed directly at Daisy. Mind you, he didn't seem to be the most gracious of men. Maybe Chloe was simply taking her cue from him.

'I would if I knew exactly who it is I'm saying hello to,' Chloe sulkily blurted.

'Oh, sorry,' Daisy replied.

'Again?' Chloe sighed, rolling her eyes.

Daisy decided to ignore the girl's rudeness and instead glanced back at Lex. 'I-I'm Daisy.'

'Daisy?' Chloe cried. 'How quaint. What's your second name? Buttercup?'

'Chloe,' her father at last said, 'don't be rude.'

Chloe regarded him, defiance evident in every stiff line of her. 'It's not rude. It was a-a statement followed by a question, that's all. I mean — ' She raked Daisy with a glance that was pure insolence. ' — who calls their daughter Daisy nowadays?'

Lex glared at her before swinging to Daisy and saying, 'I apologise for my daughter.' Chloe gave a distinct snort, but obviously decided she'd pushed her father far enough because she didn't say anything else.

'That's okay,' Daisy said. 'I was young once too, and I'm sure every bit as careless of other people's feelings.'

But her gentle reproof landed on deaf ears, because all Chloe did was turn to her sister and say, 'Come on, Imo. Let's

30

go to the Seagull caff and get a drink,' before looking back at her father and sarcastically asking, 'Is that okay with you?' She completely ignored Daisy.

'Yes, yes. I'll catch up with you.' He watched them walk away before turning back to Daisy. 'I really do apologise. Twelve is a very difficult age, or so I'm learning.' He gave her a rueful smile.

'How old is Imogen?'

'Ten. She hasn't quite mastered the art of insolence yet, but I'm sure she'll be taking lessons off her sister ready for future assaults on anyone who upsets her — which will in all probability be me.' Again he smiled ruefully, and eyed her. 'I don't think I've seen you around before, and I'm sure I would have remembered if I had.' His expression now was an admiring one, as was his tone. He seemed to have put to one side his initial annoyance at their collision.

Thank heaven Chloe's gone was Daisy's first reaction. Lord knew what spiteful comments her father's vocal appreciation would have generated. But then, to her utter dismay, she felt her face reddening. The tendency to blush in a sensitive situation was one she'd never learned to control, no matter how hard she tried, and it infuriated her each time it happened. She was positive it made her look — and it certainly made her feel — like an adolescent again; the last thing she wanted at this particular moment and in front of this supremely self-assured individual. Wasn't she old enough now to accept a compliment graciously and calmly? Her exasperation at her ineptitude intensified, with the result that her words erupted more sharply than she'd intended.

'I've only just arrived. I've taken Blue Haven for the winter.'

'Have you now?' He looked and sounded surprised; whether at her tone or at the news that she was staying at the cottage, she couldn't have said. 'Are you here with family?'

'No. I'm alone.'

He tilted his head to one side and let his gaze roam lazily over her newly coloured and shortened hair; her blue eyes, wide now as embarrassment at her girlish blushes engulfed her; her ever-so-slightly tip-tilted nose; her sculpted cheekbones; and her full lips, before moving on to her 36-24-35 figure, and lingering on the soft curve of her breasts that was so clearly visible beneath her sweater. Too late, she regretted having taken off her jacket. It would have provided some protection from those infuriatingly bold eyes.

'It's a bit on the lonely side, isn't it?' he drawled as his gaze continued to roam over her.

Daisy's blush deepened till her face felt as if it were on fire. And no wonder. Did he have to be so . . . audacious, so . . . blatant? So masculine? She could practically smell the testosterone in the air. She hoped all Cornish men weren't going to be like this.

As if to confirm her opinion of him, his glance lowered to her ringless hand. She'd long since removed her engage-ment and wedding rings, not wanting anything to remind her of her stupidity. 'No husband, I presume,' he said, 'as you're on your own.'

It wasn't a question, it was a statement. She compressed her lips, sorely tempted to tell him to mind his own business. Whether she was married or not was her affair. However, her nerve failed her, so all she managed was a low, 'That's right.' Which wasn't at all like her. She'd always been ready speak her mind; too ready at times.

He raised a quizzical eyebrow at her. Once again, she was aware of a stab of irritation. 'You don't seem sure.'

'I am.' And she was. Because, in her opinion, she wasn't married.

'No children, then?'

Again she was tempted to ask if he wanted her entire life history, but for the second time chickened out and instead said a curt, 'No.' Deciding then that he'd had his turn and that it was hers now, she smartly turned the tables on him and asked, 'And your wife? She's not with you?' She made a great play of glancing around as if searching for her.

He recognised her tactics for what they were, of course: retaliation for his nosiness. The amusement dancing in his eyes told her as surely as if he'd spoken the words out loud. 'No, we're divorced, which is why Chloe in particular is so resentful of any woman who dares to speak to me. She views her as a barrier, a threat, to my getting back with her mother. Which is what she wants more than anything. Not that that's likely to happen.'

'Well, she needn't have any worries about me. You can assure her I'm perfectly happy on my own and I have every intention of keeping things that way.' That was better, more like the confident woman Daisy had once been.

But clearly her words landed on stony ground, because something in Lex's expression, a certain gleam in his eye, told her that he didn't believe her. She tightened her lips in annoyance. He was impossibly arrogant, and judging by his present demeanour, positive that he would prove irresistible to any woman he encountered. In which case, the less she had to do with him the better. Not that she was in any danger of falling for such an overly confident man. Such glaringly obvious self-esteem repelled her.

'If you'll excuse me . . . ' she went on, unmistakably signalling her refusal to be drawn any further on the subject of her private life. Good heavens, he'd be asking her age next. ' . . . I have some shopping to get.'

'Of course. I'll go and find those daughters of mine. I hope we'll see each other again.'

Daisy shrugged, yet again having to fight the temptation to speak her mind and tell him, 'Not if I see you first.' However, her self-restraint was apparently wasted, because the corners of his mouth lifted in a maddeningly provocative half-smile, and she found herself reflecting that if she didn't know such a thing was impossible, she'd have sworn he'd read her thoughts.

'I live in Pencarrow too. Well, a couple of miles outside. We're on the Lostwithiel Road. Pencarrow Hall. Do you know it?'

'No, but then I only arrived last evening.'

'I see. Well, I'm sure we'll — uh, bump into each other.' His grin was broad and teasing. Flirtatious, even.

This time Daisy couldn't help herself. 'I'll do my best to avoid that,' she blurted.

'Oh, please don't. I'd love to repeat the experience,' he murmured, so low she almost didn't hear him. What she didn't miss, however, was the way his narrowed gaze once again swept over her. Really, was there no stopping this man? Not only was he flirting with her, but he also had the cheek of the devil. No wonder his daughter was so outspoken when she heard him speaking in such a manner.

'I'm often here in the town,' he went on. 'We could meet for a drink sometime.'

Daisy said nothing in response to that. The truth was, she had no intention of meeting him for a drink or anything else. His brazen charm wasn't going to work with her. Especially as the very last thing she intended was to get romantically involved with anyone.

'Or you could call at the Hall if you're passing. I'm usually there. I work most of the time at the house. I've set up an office. It's more convenient than commuting.'

Hah! The flames of hell would have to have been extinguished before she'd even contemplate calling on him, let alone actually do it.

'Okay. Well, I'll say goodbye for now.' He once again grinned at her, clearly not the slightest bit disheartened by her lack of enthusiasm at his invitation. But then — and Daisy didn't know why, as it certainly hadn't been her intention to encourage him in any way — she smiled back, albeit briefly.

He contemplated her for a moment before softly saying, 'You should do that more often. It suits you.' Then he swung round and simply walked away.

She stared after him. What the hell did that mean? That he found her attractive when she smiled, but not when she didn't? That he wanted her to smile at him? Grudgingly, she conceded he'd probably have no trouble at all getting women to smile at him. No wonder Chloe was so hard on any female that he spoke to. She wondered then if that was why his marriage had broken down — because he'd had a series of affairs. *And let's face it*, she thought, *if all a woman has to do is smile at him* . . . She snorted. Well, she'd take darned good care not to smile the next time she encountered him. She didn't want him getting any ideas about her availability.

★   ★   ★

By the time Daisy got back to the cottage, she was bitterly regretting having agreed to meet Freya and her friends that evening. She could be inviting all sorts of trouble. Maybe she shouldn't go. But wouldn't that be rude? She sighed.

Finally, and with great reluctance, she changed into clothes she deemed more appropriate for an evening out with friends than the sweater and jeggings she'd worn all day, and set off for Pencarrow. She'd debated driving, but with parking spaces being so limited in the town, she decided against that particular course of action and walked instead.

They'd agreed to meet at eight o'clock, so the evening was pitch black by the time she set off. Fortunately, it was mild for the end of October; it was also cloudy, which meant there wasn't even a moon to light her way. She swallowed nervously as she began to climb the hill that led up from the cottage. She was almost at the top when she wondered whether she was doing the right thing, walking alone at night. It was a fair distance into the town.

Maybe she ought to take the car, for safety's sake. She clicked her tongue impatiently. For heaven's sake, she was a grown woman, and one who'd never been afraid of the dark. She'd walk. There was absolutely nothing to be afraid of here. However, when an owl unexpectedly called from a copse of nearby trees and she leapt a couple of inches into the air, she found herself revising that conviction. Maybe the cottage was a bit too lonely for a woman on her own. She chewed at her bottom lip. It was too late now to change her mind. She'd have to make the best of it.

She quickened her step until she glimpsed the first of the streetlights just up ahead. Not much further now. She passed a large hotel, the Pencarrow; she recalled seeing it during her childhood holidays, though it was considerably smarter now. She glanced up at it. Its lights were blazing out, lessening the darkness as well as beaming a warm invitation for passers-by to go inside.

She wondered why Freya hadn't arranged to meet there. There must be a bar in a hotel of that size. Maybe she herself would suggest that another time.

Within another few minutes, Daisy was walking into the Ship. She breathed a heartfelt sigh of relief, only to immediately think, *This is pathetic*. This was a small Cornish town, one in which even at the tender age of ten she'd never felt threatened or vulnerable. But that was then and this was now, and a great deal had changed since those days.

The bar, when Daisy walked inside, was crammed with people, the buzz of their talking and laughing almost deafening beneath the low, heavily beamed ceiling. Someone called to her. It was Freya. She gingerly picked her way through the throng of drinkers to join the other woman at a table at the far side of the room.

'Daisy,' Freya greeted her. 'I've saved you a seat by me.'

Daisy sat down, then glanced round

at the other people sitting at the table. Nobody spoke; they simply stared. She felt as if she was some sort of exhibit on display for the first time. Nevertheless, she ventured a tentative smile just as Freya said, 'Right — introductions.' She tapped the shoulder of the man on her right and said, 'This is Ben, Ben Penter. Ben, meet my new friend, Daisy.'

The swarthy-skinned, good-looking man held out his hand to her and proceeded to regard her with interest. It reminded her of the way Lex Harper had looked at her, with unabashed boldness. Clearly, all Cornish men were going to be the same. Could it be something in the water or the air? All that salt and ozone? Fleetingly, she wondered if Ben was Freya's other half. Though from what she'd implied in her shop earlier that day, Daisy had assumed there wasn't anyone special in her life.

'It's good to meet you, Daisy,' Ben was saying. 'It's always nice to have a fresh face to look at, and yours is certainly worth looking at.' He grinned rakishly before cocking his head to one side and intently scrutinising her. A frown tugged at his brow. 'Have you been here before? Only I seem to know — '

Daisy hurriedly cut him off. He'd been going to say he seemed to know her. She didn't want that to be the cue for any of the others to take another look at her and then ask the same thing. 'No,' she said hurriedly. 'At least, not for twenty years. I was only ten the last time. My family and I used to come here for some of our holidays.' Her heart had begun to hammer unpleasantly hard. He'd clearly recognised something about her — from the newspaper photographs? Oh, God. If he remembered them, for sure he'd also remember the full story; and then, human nature being what it was, he'd be bound to speak of it to the other townspeople. Her cover wouldn't just be blown; it would be positively annihilated. She quickly added, 'I only arrived yesterday.'

'Oh, right.' Ben's expression remained disturbingly quizzical, however, as he asked, 'So how long are you staying?'

'For the winter, at least. Maybe longer, if I can keep the cottage. I'm at Blue Haven.'

'Yeah, Freya told us. Bit lonely, isn't it? Freya said you're on your own. Though I'm sure you won't be that way for long.' He winked at her.

Daisy breathed a tiny sigh of relief. She was out of danger, for the moment at least. But the incident, as minor as it had been, was sufficient to warn her to be always on her guard. One careless word from her was all it would take.

'Down boy,' Freya told him. 'You'll have to watch this one,' she warned Daisy. Her expression, initially a warm one, had noticeably cooled. Her eyes had narrowed even more than they were naturally; and her lips, already too thin, tightened. Once again she looked extremely plain.

It made Daisy wonder if she wasn't too far away in her speculation about a potential relationship between Ben and Freya. The signals that Freya was sending out certainly seemed to suggest that. Daisy resolved there and then not to encourage Ben. She didn't want to tread on anyone's toes; the last thing she wanted was to provoke hostility. She'd had more than enough of that recently.

'To continue,' Freya went on, 'next to Ben is Leah Bennett, also a native of Pencarrow. Leah is our resident artist. She supplies a lot of local shops with her paintings. You'll have to pay a visit to the Pencarrow Gallery at the other end of Fore Street. Her work is well worth seeing.'

Daisy looked at Leah with interest. 'I'll certainly do that. The walls of the cottage could do with something on them. They're a bit bare.'

'I'll look forward to a visit then. I'll even offer you a cup of coffee,' Leah said. 'On the house, of course.' She looked at least forty, maybe a bit older, and wore no rings, so was clearly single, at the present time at any rate. She was dressed quite differently to the others, in a long embroidered skirt and a gypsy-style off-the-shoulder blouse. Her greying hair was swept up into a brightly coloured scarf, from where it hung down her back in an intricate plait. It was a slightly old-fashioned look, but distinctive, and it suited her. The rest of the group wore jeans and sweaters. They made Daisy feel over-dressed in her linen trousers and silk blouse, though she had removed her tailored wool jacket.

'To move on,' Freya said, 'Dennis Elliot, our local hotelier. He owns the Quayside, just along the street from here. It backs onto the harbour. You can sit on the terrace and watch the boating fraternity go by with a glass of wine in your hand.'

Daisy turned her gaze to him. Like Leah, he looked older than the others; nearer fifty than forty in his case, but that could be down to his tanned, leathery complexion; due, she guessed, to over-exposure to the Cornish weather. Single? It seemed likely. He wore no rings on his hands. She'd hazard a guess that this was a regular get-together for people on their own. In which case, she mused, she would fit in perfectly.

'I passed it this morning,' Daisy said to Freya. 'It looks very exclusive.' And very expensive.

Dennis nodded his head at her but didn't speak. His expression, unlike Ben's, was shuttered and unreadable; his eyes were the colour of pewter and strangely opaque. Daisy couldn't help but wonder if he also thought he knew her. Her heartbeat quickened for the second time as her stomach lurched with a sick feeling of dread. This wasn't going to work. She should never have come here. Whatever had she been thinking? A large town, or even a city, would have been a much better choice. She would have blended in with the many thousands of other residents and never been noticed. Now, as a new face in a small community, she stood out like a fox in a hen coop. Which meant she was in very real danger of being recognised.

'Okay,' Freya said, 'the introductions are over. Who wants another drink? Daisy, what can I get you? You've waited long enough.'

But Daisy wasn't listening, because she had just spotted Lex Harper walking into the bar with a strikingly beautiful woman. Which shouldn't be surprising. It was, after all, exactly what Daisy expected of him in the wake of their encounter that morning.

3

'Hah! I see you've clocked our resident Casanova,' Freya gleefully said.

'Yes,' Daisy said. 'Actually, I bumped into him outside your shop this morning.' It occurred to her that Freya's description wouldn't just apply to Lex Harper; Ben would certainly qualify. There'd been a distinctly flirtatious manner to him. He clearly liked women.

'Did you? Did you speak to him?'

'Well — yes. I had to, really.'

'What did you say?'

'Sorry.'

'I said, what did you — '

'Sorry is what I said to him. I wasn't looking where I was going. It was my fault entirely.'

'You literally bumped into him, then?'

Daisy nodded and grimaced wryly. 'I all but knocked him into the road. But for his quick action — '

But Freya didn't let her finish. 'What did he say?' She was looking annoyed, if her frown and the tightening of her mouth for a second time was anything to go by. But what could have annoyed her? The fact that Daisy had bumped into Lex? Apologised to him? Conceded, in fact, that she was to blame?

'Well, nothing to start with. He was too intent on holding on to me, stopping me from stumbling and dropping my bag of glass. Stopping us both, in fact, from ending up lying in the road. He was very nice about it.' Nice? That was a joke. Yet for some reason, she was reluctant to tell Freya what had actually taken place between them — the initial sarcasm, followed by the provocative and outrageously flirtatious behaviour.

However, she didn't need to say any more, because Freya echoed her thoughts exactly by scoffing, 'Nice? Nice?' before loudly hooting with laughter.

Daisy cringed, mainly because several people had glanced their way, their curiosity plain to see. The last thing she wanted was to become the focal point of the entire pub. She huddled down in her seat and was even tempted to seek refuge under the table, so desperate was she to avoid people's attention. And she'd thought she'd left these sorts of feelings behind her. A sense of hopelessness and despair filled her. Would she ever again experience the confidence she'd once known; that she'd lost over the past couple of months?

But Freya didn't notice any of this. 'Lex Harper's more than nice. He's bloody gorgeous. And as rich as Croesus into the bargain.'

'Ssh,' Leah cautioned. 'He'll hear you, for goodness sake. Oh my God, he's coming over. He must have heard you. You and your big mouth, Freya.'

Freya, completely unconcerned by Leah's exasperation with her, glanced across the room, as did Daisy. Sure enough, Lex Harper was heading their way. What made the whole thing worse was the fact that his gaze was fixed firmly upon Daisy. Oh, good grief, he didn't think it had been her speaking so loudly about him, did he?

'Hi,' he said to her as he approached the table. 'I see you've made yourself at home here.' His expression was one of bemusement. He then glanced around the table at the other occupants, his gaze lingering on the two men.

Ben took the lead. 'Hi, I'm Ben Penter, and this is Dennis Elliot.'

Dennis nodded. He still hadn't uttered a single word. Daisy was beginning to wonder if he could actually speak.

'Do you know Leah?' Ben went on. 'She's a very talented artist. And this is — ?'

'How nice to see you, Lex,' Freya chipped in before Ben could introduce her.

Lex was beginning to look a little confused. 'Uh, I don't — '

'It's Freya Carne? I own the glass shop in Fore Street.'

Daisy stared at Freya. The woman's cheeks were bright pink, and her eyes were shining. Daisy belatedly understood her keen interest in what had happened between herself and Lex. Freya was attracted to him.

'Oh, yes,' Lex said, 'I bumped into Daisy outside this morning. I don't think I've ever been inside.'

'You have,' Freya smartly corrected him. 'About . . . ooh, now let me see . . . three months ago. You bought a pendant for someone.'

She was practically batting her eyelids now, Daisy saw, and all but simpering, forcing Daisy to suppress the chuckle that was steadily rising in her throat. Such behaviour seemed totally out of character for the plain-speaking woman Freya had initially appeared to be.

'Ah, yes, I remember now,' Lex said. 'A birthday gift for my daughter, Chloe. Sorry, you'll have to forgive my appalling memory.' He swept his gaze back to Daisy. 'Well, it's nice to see you again, Daisy.' His eyes gleamed. 'As I said this morning, I'll hope to, uh — bump into you again very soon.'

Daisy chose not to respond to that piece of innuendo. She just hoped nobody else had picked up on his meaning.

'Lex, darling.' It was his lovely companion. She'd walked across the room, clearly intent on dragging Lex back to her. 'Are you going to buy me a drink or not?' She totally ignored the other people round the table.

Lex swivelled his head and looked at her. 'Sorry, Andrea. That was rude of me, walking away like that.'

'It was, rather,' she agreed. 'Won't you introduce me?' Her blue eyes were steely enough to cut through paper as she took in the small group; in particular, when she directed her gaze to the women.

'Oh, well, this is Daisy, a recent arrival in the town, and um, Freya, wasn't it?'

Freya blushed an even deeper crimson. Daisy suspected that it was due to her indignation at Lex's offhand manner towards her rather than another attempt to coyly flirt. It was evident she'd hoped to make more of an impression on him than she had.

He swept his glance to Leah then. 'And this is Leah.'

Freya, obviously still keen to hold his attention, cut in at this point, 'Our local artist.'

Andrea contributed nothing to this exchange. She was manifestly not impressed with any of them.

'Well,' Lex went on, 'have a good evening.' He again turned to Daisy as if about to say something else, but before he could do so, Andrea slipped her arm through his.

'Come along, Lex, she said. 'I'm starving.'

He gave a rueful smile, raised his eyebrows, and the two of them walked away into what looked like another room.

'What's in there?' Daisy asked.

'A small restaurant,' Freya muttered. 'What on earth's he doing with *her*? I thought he had better taste than that.'

'What's wrong with her?'

Freya snorted. 'Other than being a tramp, do you mean?'

'Tramp? That's the last thing she looked like.'

'Huh,' Freya scoffed. 'Fancy clothes do not a lady make.'

Andrea had indeed been beautifully dressed and exquisitely made up. Her long, silky-smooth blonde hair had been to die for in Daisy's opinion. If only her own had behaved as well when it was longer, instead of flying about all over the place, no matter how much styling mousse and lacquer she applied to it. Of course, now it was short it was much easier to manage. But she'd always dreamed of having long, satin-smooth hair, the sort that looked as if it had been ironed.

'So she's local?' Daisy said.

'If you can call Lostwithiel local,' Freya replied. 'Her husband got fed up with her playing away from home and left her. Or at least, that's what the rumour mill says. She's obviously got her painted talons into Lex. I would have thought he'd have had more sense. And what that termagant of a daughter of his will say, I can't imagine.' She snorted disparagingly. 'I'd like to be a fly on that particular wall when she finds out.'

Daisy absently nodded. 'Ye-es, I met her too this morning. She's called Chloe.' She recalled the girl's muttered, 'Not another one.'

Freya regarded her in surprise. 'Did you?'

'Yes, and the younger girl, Imogen. Chloe does seem possessive of her father.'

'From what I've heard, she's hell-bent on getting Lex and her mother back together. But again, from what I've heard, that's not going to happen.' She snorted once more. 'She's shacked up with some wealthy guy — a multi-millionaire, if what I've heard is right. An IT tycoon; real high-flyer.'

Daisy wondered where Freya had heard all of this. The town was obviously a hotbed of gossip. And that fact didn't do anything to lessen her dread of being recognised. Again, she wondered what the hell had possessed her to come to a small seaside town where everyone knew everything about everyone else. If the other residents were anything like Freya, they'd soon ferret out the truth. She began to feel sick.

'He's got houses all over the world,' Freya was saying, completely oblivious to Daisy's sudden pallor. 'His own plane, yacht . . . you name it, he's got it. She's not likely to walk away from all of that, is she?'

'Lex is pretty rich, though, isn't he?' Daisy managed to speak with some semblance of calm. 'He must be if he owns Pencarrow Hall. I haven't seen it, but it sounds very substantial.'

'Oh he is, and yes, Pencarrow Hall's a large house. Well, it's a manor house, really. But, for all that, he's not quite in the same league as Hank Sinclair, although he's catching up pretty quickly if the rumours are true. Haven't you heard of Hank? You must have.' She glanced at Daisy, her expression one of superiority. 'He's regularly splashed over the newspapers.'

Daisy shook her head. 'No, I haven't. So what split Lex and his wife up? Do you know?'

'Yes. She's called Annabel, by the way. She was playing away. Well, both of them were.'

Where did she get all this information from? Daisy wondered if there was there some sort of telegraph system in operation in the town. 'So why would you be interested in a man like that?' she asked Freya. 'Because clearly you are.'

'Hah! You noticed.' Freya laughed.

'Yes.'

'Not treading on your toes, am I?' Freya slanted a glance at her.

'Good grief, no. He's not my type.'

'Not your type?' Freya gave another hoot. 'He's got a soddin' great house, servants at his beck and call, expensive cars. Does quite a lot of travelling. I've heard he's got a house in France somewhere too. Provence, I think.'

'How do you know all this?'

'Keep my ear — and my nose — alert.' She tapped those particular parts of her anatomy with her index finger. 'You hear a lot that way.'

'Clearly you have,' Daisy archly replied.

Freya looked at her, one eyebrow raised, her expression one of indignation. 'And why not?' she demanded, obviously sensing some sort of slur upon her motives for gathering local news. 'What's wrong with keeping abreast of local affairs? As in affairs, literally. Believe me, they're all at it. In fact, half the people in town are having affairs with the other half.' She gave a snort of contempt. 'I mean, you've just seen Lex with another woman. What more evidence do you want?'

'He's divorced, Freya,' Daisy quietly put in. 'He's doing nothing wrong.' But she couldn't help asking herself, was he? And was Andrea divorced, or simply unhappy? In an effort to move the topic of conversation away from local affairs — or gossip, as she considered it — she asked, 'What does he do to earn all this money?'

'Oh, he has fingers in all sorts of pies. I suppose he could be described as an entrepreneur. He owns several factories; he's big in property development. That's where he made the bulk of his money. His company, Harper Enterprises, built the new leisure centre between here and Bodmin. He owns a string of hotels all over the south, one of which is the Pencarrow, on the Esplanade. He's loaded.'

'Money's not everything,' Daisy said. And she could certainly attest to that. 'Anyway, he can't be that wonderful if his wife left him.' She paused. 'Do the two girls live with him?'

'A lot of the time, yeah. Their mother's always off with her new husband, travelling. Word has it — '

Again? Daisy mused.

' — that he doesn't want to be encumbered with someone else's daughters, certainly not Chloe.'

'You know that, do you?'

'Well, I've not actually had it from the horse's mouth . . . ' For the first time, Freya looked uncertain. It didn't last, however. She glared defensively at Daisy. 'Anyway, I've lived here long enough to get to know most of what goes on. You've been here for two minutes.'

A bit longer than that, Daisy mused. She said nothing, however. She had no wish to pour petrol onto an already inflamed situation.

'What are you two in a huddle about?' It was Ben.

'Nothing you'd be interested in,' Freya said.

'Nose a bit out of joint, is it?' Ben slanted a glance at Daisy. 'She's got a thing about Lex Harper. Trouble is, I don't think it's reciprocated.'

'And how would you know anyway?' Freya angrily retaliated.

'I don't. It's just a feeling. In fact, I'd say his sights are firmly set elsewhere.' He slid his twinkling glance towards Daisy.

Thankfully, Freya didn't seem to

have picked up on his meaning, but Daisy knew exactly what he was implying. Lex had seemed very interested in her. She hastily buried her nose in her glass and gulped her wine down. If he was, he was on to a loser as far as she was concerned. As she'd already decided, there was no way she'd allow herself to become involved with someone like him. She intended to steer well clear of men for the foreseeable future; she'd learnt her lesson. But if she did ever decide it was time to form some sort of relationship, it would be with an ordinary man, someone like — she glanced across the table to see Ben still surreptitiously watching her, as was Dennis — someone like Ben.

He saw her looking at him and winked. She grinned back, and for the first time that evening began to feel at ease, despite the way Dennis was still regarding her. He couldn't be interested in her, surely? Other than maybe wondering whether he knew her. And that suspicion was all it took to resurrect her feelings of fear and apprehension.

An hour later, Daisy made her excuses and left the Ship. It was a good twenty-minute walk back to Blue Haven and she didn't want to leave it too late. The Esplanade, when she reached it, was eerily deserted. She shivered and pulled her jacket closer around her. Nervously, she regarded the road ahead of her. It disappeared into total darkness a bit further along where the street lighting petered out. There wasn't even any moonlight to make her feel a little better. So it wasn't all that surprising that when she heard the sound of footsteps somewhere behind her, she instinctively quickened her own step. Lex's hotel was just up ahead. If she could just make that . . .

'Daisy, for God's sake, slow up, will you?'

She looked back. It was Ben.

'I didn't like the idea of you walking all that way alone,' he added breathlessly.

She wasn't sure how she felt about

him walking her back. His attraction to her had clearly heightened as the evening had worn on, and what was more, he'd made no attempt to hide it. Perhaps she should tell him the truth — that she wasn't really and truly free. But if she did that, he'd be bound to ask questions, and she couldn't risk that; it could inadvertently jog his memory. She'd never been good at deceiving people. The few times she'd attempted it, she'd instantly given herself away, especially to her mother. So why on earth did she think she'd get away with it now?

'I'll be fine,' she insisted. 'It's not that far. I'll have to get used to it if I'm going to stay here.'

'Well, now I'm here I may as well walk you back. Don't worry — ' He gave her a roguish grin. ' — I'll be on my very best behaviour.'

She couldn't help but smile back. 'I won't be treading on anyone else's toes if I let you do that, will I?'

'If you mean Freya, no, definitely

not. She's got her sights fixed considerably higher than me, a mere fisherman
— as I'm sure you noticed tonight.' He
clearly meant Lex Harper. 'Not that
she'll get anywhere with him. Look,
Daisy,' he began, slightly hesitantly,
'watch out for him. He's the ruthless
type, I've heard.'

Oh, good Lord, not more gossip,
Daisy wearily thought. Did the people
here do nothing but talk about others?
It didn't bode well for her if they were
this inquisitive. She sighed.

'What's that sigh for?' Ben asked.

'Oh, you know.'

'I don't. Tell me.'

'It's nothing, really.'

He eyed her, his head cocked to
one side. 'Well, I'll just say it again
— Harper's the predatory sort, too sure
of himself by half.'

'Ben, believe me, there's no need to
worry. He's the very last type of man
I'd ever be interested in.'

His eyebrow lifted. 'Had your fingers
burned then?'

'You could say that.'

The same eyebrow went even higher.

'Not by him. By someone else. That's why I'm here. I-I need some breathing space. I've no intention of getting involved with anyone.' And that was all she was going to say.

Ben raised his hands in the air. 'Okay, okay, I get the message, loud and clear.'

'We-ell, as long as you understand.'

'I do. I can always hope, though.'

'There's no point, really.'

'Well, can I at least hold your hand? In a purely platonic way, of course.'

She laughed then, really laughed. 'You're hopeless.'

'I know. It's a lovable trait, wouldn't you say?'

So that's what they did. They walked and talked, laughed and joked, and throughout it all their fingers remained entwined. And Daisy had to admit, it was comforting to have him with her. Especially when they passed the hotel, and she saw Lex Harper standing at a window, looking down at them. She hadn't spotted him leaving the pub. There must be a back exit. He raised a hand in greeting. Daisy pretended not to notice.

4

As it turned out, she needn't have worried. Ben proved to be a true gentleman, leaving her at her front door with nothing more demanding than a brush of his lips on her cheek.

'I'll see you around, my girl,' he said. 'No pressure, but I'm here if you need a friend. I might even take you fishing if you're interested.'

She pulled a face. 'Not really my scene.'

'Have you ever tried it?'

'Once, twenty years ago with my father.'

'Things have changed a bit since then. Still, we'll see.' And with a cheerful wave, he left.

Daisy watched him as he disappeared up the hill, then she opened the door of the cottage and stepped inside. She switched on all the lights as she went in so that each room was bathed in brightness, the dark corners and shadows banished. It helped to also banish her feeling of loneliness, as for the umpteenth time she wondered whether she'd done the right thing in moving this far away from her family.

★ ★ ★

An unexpected noise woke Daisy in the night. It sounded like someone banging hard on the front door. She even thought she heard the sound of the handle being turned. She sat up in bed, heart pounding fiercely, her senses on high alert. However, when she heard nothing else she decided she'd been dreaming and lay back down, closing her eyes once more.

Until it happened again.

This time, the noise was even louder. It sounded like a fist hammering over and over. She sprang up. Was someone trying to break in? But why warn her by banging on the door first? She switched on the bedside light and climbed out of bed, grabbing her dressing gown from the hook on the back of the door and sliding her arms into it, before tying the belt securely around her waist. Somehow, that simple action made her feel less vulnerable to harm. She crept onto the landing and listened again; she could hear nothing. Determined to check everything out, she moved to the window that looked down onto the road. No one was out there. Surely she couldn't have imagined it? Or dreamt it, for a second time?

Gingerly, she then crept down the stairs. Could it be Ben? Had he returned for some reason? She paused on the bottom step and switched on the hall light. The first thing she noticed was the white envelope lying on the carpet. She crossed to it and picked it up. Who the hell would be delivering a letter in the middle of the night?

She looked down at it and gasped in horror, her stomach lurching wildly as she saw that her worst fear had been realised.

The name printed on the front was Darcey Carter.

'No . . . oh no. How — ?'

She ripped the envelope open and pulled out the single sheet of paper that was neatly folded inside. The words on it were printed in large black capital letters. Her gaze skimmed them, and her entire body began to shake.

YES, I KNOW WHO YOU REALLY ARE AND I KNOW WHAT YOU DID. WHY DON'T YOU COME CLEAN AND PAY BACK THE MONEY TO ALL THE PEOPLE YOU STOLE FROM? IF YOU DON'T, I'M GOING TO GO PUBLIC WITH YOUR TRUE IDENTITY.

She crumpled it up in her fist, pressing her other hand hard against her mouth. Someone had recognised her, just as she'd feared they would. She groaned in despair. She knew she shouldn't have agreed to go out tonight. Why had she? It couldn't be coincidence that this had happened right afterwards. She should have listened to her instincts.

This had to be the work of one of the people she'd met. Ben? He'd thought he recognised her. Had he finally recalled where he'd seen her before? Had it happened while he'd been walking her home? Or Dennis — could it be him? He'd spent a large part of the evening stealing glances at her.

She gave a trembling sob as something even more disturbing occurred to her. Could whoever it was still be out there? Should she open the door and look? Did she have the courage? Or should she phone the police? But then she'd have to explain, show them the letter and confess the truth, and she didn't want to do that. Even in the police force, things could leak out. And as at the moment it appeared that only the person who'd written this knew the truth, wouldn't it be wiser to remain silent?

Coming to a decision, she darted to the door and unlocked it, then cracked it open an inch. She put one eye to the gap and peered out. As far as she could see — which actually wasn't all that far — the road was deserted. She opened the door wider and bravely thrust her head out. No one was there. Not that she could see much; there still wasn't any moonlight and the night was pitch black. Should she venture out and try to follow whoever it was? But supposing they were out there somewhere, waiting for her? Swiftly, she slammed the door closed and stood with her back pressed against it for several minutes.

She then ran into the kitchen and stared through the window. Her tears flowed, blinding her. Which was why she didn't see the person standing, silent and unmoving, in the deep shadows beneath the branches of a tree to the left of the cottage. The figure watched for several more moments until Daisy moved away from the window; it then darted out and sprinted up the hill, back towards Pencarrow.

A cup of tea, Daisy decided; she needed a cup of tea. At four thirty in the morning, there was no point returning to bed. She'd never sleep. Not after what had happened. In fact, she found herself wondering if she'd ever sleep again.

How could this have happened? She might as well have stayed where she was and moved in with her parents.

She switched the kettle on and sat down at the small table, burying her face in her hands. They were still trembling, as much with shock as fear. So her identity had been uncovered, and if she didn't do what the letter said, everyone in the town would know.

With that, the memories flooded back in all their graphic horror — the nightmarish events of those last few weeks in the Lancashire seaside town of Formby. The discovery of what her husband, Grant, had been doing. Precisely how he'd acquired the immense wealth that had changed their lifestyle so rapidly from ordinary middle-class to extreme luxury. The papers had called it a Ponzi-type scheme. She'd never even heard of such a thing. She'd simply accepted Grant's explanation that he'd made some very profitable investments. Even when he'd bought the large house, the expensive car, the yacht, and the jewellery, she still hadn't questioned it. How stupid she'd been. How gullible. How blind.

The newspapers had swiftly gathered all the facts, put them together, and published them. Grant had persuaded large numbers of people all over the country to invest their money with him — huge amounts, in some cases entire life savings — with the promise of fast and substantial rewards. In reality, he'd made no investments at all. He'd simply paid people their supposed profits out of new money that he received, until in the end it all grew too big, and the only thing he could do to avoid arrest and imprisonment was to abscond with the fortune he'd managed to salt away — leaving Darcey, his wife, to face the public condemnation alone. No matter how often she protested that she had known nothing about any of it, no one believed her.

'She must have known,' the papers had written. 'How could she not have? Where did she think all the money had come from?' The media went into a frenzy. Reporters camped outside her house, their cameras whirring and flashing whenever they spotted her. And soon, photographs of her face had been splashed alongside Grant's in all the national newspapers, so that in his absence she'd been the one who'd been subjected to the unending torrent of abuse and threats; threats that had forced her to leave all that she loved and run away. All to no avail.

She gave another small sob. The truth was she had no idea where Grant was. Abroad, she guessed, far away from the risk of prosecution. There'd been no word from him. Not that she'd expected any. They'd been growing apart for a while. In fact, she'd begun to suspect he was having an affair; several, probably. And he'd made no secret of his sudden wealth and profligate spending. Such behaviour, such blatant extravagance, would be bound to attract a certain type of woman.

It wasn't until he'd gone that Darcey discovered that only a few of his recently acquired possessions had actually been fully paid for, so almost everything, apart from her jewellery and some furniture, had been repossessed, along with the house. Fortunately, he'd been relatively generous with Darcey too, telling her to 'spend, spend, spend. There's plenty more where that came from.' And she had spent a large proportion of it, mainly on designer clothes, at Grant's bidding. 'You have to look like the wife of a rich man,' he'd tell her, adding scornfully, 'Not like some little suburban hausfrau.' So, not surprisingly, she hadn't got all that much money left. Enough, with the things she'd managed to sell, to rent Blue Haven and live on for a while. Maybe she should try and return that to Grant's victims. But, she agonised, what difference would it make? It was such a tiny proportion of what Grant had stolen that it hardly seemed worthwhile. But so great and unrelenting had been the hatred and venom directed at her personally, that she'd been forced to not only move away but also to change her appearance and her name. So Darcey Carter became Daisy Lewis, Lewis being her maiden name.

One thing she was grateful for was the fact that Grant had never tried to persuade her father to invest with him. Unlikely as it seemed, he must have had some sort of conscience.

The kettle boiled and she made her tea. She then sat for what remained of the night, drinking cup after cup, until she felt ready to burst. But she had made a decision.

She was damned if she was going to let someone drive her away again. She'd done nothing wrong. Nothing. If it came to it, she'd have to make people believe that.

By the time dawn had broken, she'd made another decision. She had to find out who was responsible for the night's events. And to do that, she'd need to stay alert and listen carefully to everything that anyone said to her. Search their expressions and their glances for any sign of resentment or hatred. But above all, she had to stay on her guard. Who knew what this person would be capable of? Some sort of physical retribution, as well as broadcasting her real name? Would they be prepared to actually harm her if she didn't pay up? It seemed a very real threat.

It was obviously someone who'd lost their money and wanted it back. If they only knew she hadn't got it — or, at least, nowhere near enough, because the total amount lost ran into the millions of pounds, apparently. But that admission didn't quieten the fast beating of her heart or the lurching sensation of sick dread in her stomach. If only she had someone with her; someone she could trust. Someone who would help her survive this ordeal.

A dog. Yes, that was it. She'd get a dog. A large dog. Not only would it be company, but she'd feel safer too. Why hadn't she thought of it before? But would the owner of the house allow that? She'd ask the estate agent; he'd know. In fact, she'd go this morning, as soon as she'd had some breakfast.

But despite her good intentions, as soon as she tried to eat the bowl of fruit and yogurt she'd prepared, her stomach heaved, and she ended up throwing it all into the bin. Minutes later, she was on her way into the town.

The morning was a fresh one, the wind blowing straight off the sea. She could hear the thud of the waves as they struck the rocks that edged Sandy Cove and then crept onward up the beach. She huddled down into her jacket and pulled the collar up about her neck and chin. This, then, was a taste of what she could expect as winter progressed. She stopped halfway up the hill and looked down onto Blue Haven. She couldn't have chosen a more exposed place to live, though the cliffs that rose from and edged the cove, thereby forming the headland, would afford some protection, she supposed. She turned and walked on, looking forward to mingling with the town's inhabitants.

But Pencarrow, when she reached it, was deserted. There were one or two individuals darting in and out of the shops, but the chill of the morning had clearly kept people indoors. The estate agent's was also empty, apart from a single woman sitting behind a desk. She glanced up as Daisy walked in and with a smile said, 'Good morning. How can I help you?'

'I'm renting Blue Haven for the winter, and well, I was wondering whether I could have a dog for company. It's a bit lonely out there. Would the owner be agreeable, do you think?'

'Oh.' The woman looked uncertain. 'I'm just the part-time assistant, and I'm fairly new at that. I'll call the manager, Mr Whitman. If you could just bear with me for a moment, he might know.'

She disappeared through the doorway behind the desk.

Several minutes later, the man whom Daisy had first seen when she'd arrived in Pencarrow appeared, the woman right behind him. 'Ah, Ms Lewis.' He beamed. 'Josie has told me about your request, and I've phoned the owner, but I'm afraid his policy is strictly no pets. I had hoped that as you're a long let he would be more amenable to the idea, but I'm afraid not. Sorry.' He shrugged, his expression one of sympathy.

'Oh.' Daisy's earlier feeling of excitement faded as agonising disappointment took its place. She'd been keenly imagining a dog walking at her side, lying at her feet in the evening, greeting her in the morning, but it wasn't to be. 'Well, never mind.'

'I'm really sorry.'

'Yes, so am I. A dog would have been some company. Still, I'll get used to being alone, I suppose.' But would she? Especially now, in the light of the letter she'd received and the disturbance of the night before? She could only hope that if she didn't react to the threat — in other words, ignored it — whoever it had been would decide that any further action would be futile. However, she wasn't banking on that. The wording of the letter had been very explicit — pay up or else. It had been glaringly obvious that the writer meant business.

Feeling very downcast, she decided she may as well do some shopping while she was in town. And she'd take a look at the gallery that Leah had told her about; maybe find a painting to hang on the sitting-room wall. Apart from a couple of small framed prints, it was otherwise bare. She hoped Leah would be there. She'd claim that promised cup of coffee if she was. Anything to divert her thoughts from the blackmailer.

Her luck was in. Leah was there, and she looked positively ecstatic to see Daisy. Though Daisy hadn't considered that her night-time visitor could have been a woman, she now found herself wondering if it could have been Leah. She had, after all, been one of the people she'd met the previous evening. Yet, surely she wouldn't greet Daisy this warmly if it had been her. There'd be some indication of resentment, embarrassment, shame maybe, at being face to face with her victim, wouldn't there? But then again, given her lack of any sort of suspicion about Grant and the sheer number of his expensive acquisitions, could Daisy rely on her instincts about people anymore?

'You found me, then.'

'Yes.' Daisy looked around. Like the town had been, the gallery was empty of people; the walls, however, were filled with the most spectacular artwork. 'Oh, these are gorgeous.'

Leah smiled, genuinely gratified by Daisy's praise. 'Thank you. Have a look round while I make us some coffee. I take it you want one?'

'Yes, please.' Reassured by Leah's good-natured invitation, Daisy smiled back and started to walk around the room. She had to trust someone, otherwise she'd go mad. And Leah looked too friendly, too guileless, too open, to behave in such a cruel manner to anyone.

'You'll see they're all priced. Not that I'm pressing you to buy one.' Leah grinned broadly, once again demonstrating a complete absence of any sort of rancour or resentment.

Daisy slowly wandered from painting to painting, her coffee cup in her hand, before finally settling on a view of the harbour from the town quay. The style was what was described nowadays as naive, but the colours were wonderful, and greatly exaggerated in their richness though somehow they worked. Leah even gave her a ten-percent discount. 'As you're a friend,' she said. 'Now, sit down and tell me how you're getting on at Blue Haven. It would be too lonely for me.'

'I have to admit it is for me, too, which is why I thought about having a dog.'

'Only thought?'

'Yeah, and I've been told by the owner of the cottage that I can't have one.'

'That's a shame. It would have been marvellous company for you, as well as a good excuse for lots of lovely long walks.'

'Oh, I can have those without a dog.'

'Mind you . . . ' Out of the blue, Leah suddenly looked devious. ' . . . would they know if you got one anyway?'

Daisy stared at her, her previous certainty about Leah's trustworthiness shaken by this unexpected evidence of slyness; of duplicity. But surely her visitor of the night before couldn't be a woman? No woman would behave in that way . . . would she? Walking about in the middle of the night, alone? Belatedly, it seemed highly improbable. Yet, if she'd lost a great deal of money and was hoping to get it back, *needed* to get it back, would it be beyond the realms of possibility to resort to such tactics?

Daisy thrust her suspicions to one side, silently reiterating the fact that she mustn't automatically distrust everyone she encountered, or she'd end up with no friends at all; no one she could grow close to. And that was unthinkable. Also, if Leah was the person responsible for the letter, would she be encouraging Daisy to get a dog? Again, it seemed unlikely.

'Oh, I don't think I could.'

'You do know who owns Blue Haven, don't you?'

'No.'

'A very close friend of Lex Harper's. Maybe a word in his ear — ?' Leah cheekily winked at her, her meaning all too clear: Daisy should ask Lex to put in a word on her behalf. Could she bring herself to do that?

'Do you think he'd help me?'

'Well,' Leah went on, 'he certainly looked very taken with you last evening. Why not give him a call and ask him? If you don't ask, you don't get.'

'Would his phone number be in the

directory? I'd have thought he'd be ex-directory. You know, being such a wealthy and prominent businessman.'

'Let's have a look, shall we?' Leah pulled out a weighty-looking phone directory from beneath her desk. A swift look, however, drew a blank, just as Daisy had predicted. 'Hmm, now who'd know, I wonder? Of course, you could go and simply knock on his door.'

'Oh no, I couldn't.'

'Why not? I'm sure he'd be pleased to see you. He more or less said that last night in the pub. He might even invite you inside.' She winked again. 'And who knows what that might lead to?'

Daisy gave a snort of laughter. 'You're outrageous.'

'I know, but it's worth a try, isn't it? Do you know his address?'

'Yes, he told me.'

'He told you!' Leah cried. 'Well, there you are then. It's practically an invitation, which means he must want you to call in.'

'I don't know.' Daisy regarded her doubtfully.

'Go on. Live dangerously.'

Live dangerously? Daisy reflected. She'd been doing that for the past two months, and she wanted no more of it.

'You can't miss it,' Leah went on. 'It's the house on the right as you approach the first T-junction you come to.'

'I really don't think I could just turn up on his doorstep.'

'Yes, you can. Go on, go for it. I dare you.'

5

Daisy thought about Leah's words all the way home. Lex had said to call in if she was ever passing that way. And the truth was, now that she'd thought about having a dog, she found she quite desperately wanted one. To bestow a feeling of security, if nothing else.

By the time she reached Blue Haven, her painting tucked under her arm, she'd decided she'd leave it a few more days, maybe even a week, and then call at Pencarrow Hall. She didn't want to appear overeager, or worse still, pushy. Though she did have a legitimate and highly plausible reason for visiting, she'd hate Lex to think she had any other motive, such as inviting him into some sort of relationship with her. Maybe she shouldn't go.

But two nights later, as if to extinguish her bouts of indecision and replace them with a single-minded determination, the house phone rang and a muffled voice that could have belonged to anyone, male or female, said, 'Did you read my note? If I were you, I wouldn't ignore it. This isn't going to stop until you and your husband repay the money you stole.'

Before she could reply, however, the call was cut off. Which was ridiculous, because even if she had the funds necessary to repay such a huge amount of money, she wouldn't know how to go about it. The caller would need to provide her with some way of handing over the money. Otherwise, what was the purpose of it all?

What it did do, though, was make her decide there and then to pay her visit to Pencarrow Hall the very next day. It was essential that she have a dog, a companion who'd hopefully protect her in the event of a physical attack. And if the only way to achieve that was to ask Lex Harper to help her, then that was what she'd do.

Daisy promptly dialled 1471 and, as she'd expected, was told there was no number to return the call. But that wasn't the end of it. The phone proceeded to ring at half-hourly intervals throughout the night. In the end, she stopped picking up. No one had spoken after the first time. The caller obviously just wanted to frighten and intimidate her. Persecute her, even.

Once again, she ate no breakfast, so eager was she to be on her way to the Hall. She made herself wait, however. She couldn't go calling at eight o'clock in the morning. By nine o'clock, though, her impatience was such that she could wait no longer, and she left the house, making sure all the windows were closed and fastened, before carefully locking the door behind her. Her car was parked right next to the cottage in the small parking bay, which meant that as she started towards it she could hear the phone ringing yet again. She groaned. How long was this going to continue? Surely if she didn't answer, whoever it was would get fed up.

She had no trouble finding Lex's house. Though tall gates guarded the entrance to the drive and equally high iron palings flanked them for some distance, the house was perfectly visible from the road. She climbed from the car and tried the gates. To her surprise, they weren't locked and opened easily. She got back into the car and slowly negotiated the gently curving driveway.

Manicured lawns stretched out on either side of her as far as she could see, punctuated here and there by large geometrically shaped beds of ornamental shrubs and flowers, as well as several groupings of what looked like birch, oak, and beech trees, both the green and the copper. It was all expertly laid out, shapes and colours contrasting one against the other perfectly. It suggested that Lex had had the design of the grounds planned and executed by someone of considerable skill and expertise.

The house was also impressive, and

appeared more so the closer she got to it. A steeply sloping slate roof topped granite-grey walls, their intimidating severity mitigated only by rows of mullioned windows. She parked at the foot of a flight of shallow stone steps and regarded the massive oak door with deep misgiving. Should she go and ring the bell that she could see there, or should she just leave? It didn't look like the sort of house whose inhabitants would welcome casual callers.

She wavered back and forth between the two options before finally getting out and moving towards the steps. But then her resolve once again failed her, and she stopped halfway across. She couldn't do this; she just couldn't. Not even to be able to own a dog. What would he think of her calling at this time of the morning? No matter that he'd invited her to. People said these things, but didn't imagine you'd actually take them up on it. She'd done the very same thing herself on several occasions.

Making up her mind, she swung back towards the car. Someone must know his phone number; it was just a question of discovering who.

'Daisy? Is that you?'

She swivelled and saw Lex standing in the open doorway, looking down at her. 'Y-yes. I-I was — '

'How wonderful to see you. Please, come in, won't you? I was about to go out in a moment or two, but I can make other arrangements.'

'Dad, who is it?' a girl's voice called, right before Chloe appeared behind him. If Daisy could have run away then without appearing foolish, she undoubtedly would have. For the girl's expression, just as it had been on their first encounter, was one of utter contempt as she spotted who it was her father was speaking to. Daisy had expected her to be at school or she never would have come.

'It's Daisy. You remember her?'

'Oh yes, I remember her. What do you want?' she rudely demanded.

'Chloe! That's enough,' Lex chided.

'Aren't you going out?'

'Yeah, Imogen and I are meeting Mum. She'll be very interested to hear about this.'

'I'm sure she won't,' Lex riposted curtly. 'Where is your sister?'

'She's just coming.'

'Right. Oh, there you are, darling.' Imogen appeared and also looked disturbed to see Daisy. 'Call Mrs Sutton. She'll drive you.'

'Why can't you?' Chloe demanded. 'Last night you said you would.'

'I said I might, but now I have a visitor.'

'I'll go. I shouldn't have called.' Daisy had never felt so embarrassed. 'It was just a chance call. I-I wanted to ask for your help.'

'I bet you did,' Chloe sneered. 'What's happened?' She glanced beyond Daisy. 'Has your nasty little car broken down conveniently on our driveway?'

'Chloe, I won't tell you again, that's enough,' Lex firmly rebuked her. 'Now go and find Mrs Sutton.'

Daisy felt she should say something to try and put matters right. She certainly didn't want Lex and his daughter falling out over her. Such a thing wouldn't endear her to Chloe; far from it. Though why that should bother her, she didn't know. After today she doubted she'd have anything more to do with Lex Harper. Why would she? They moved in completely different worlds; his was one of wealth and luxury, while hers was one of deception and now fear.

'No, m-my car hasn't broken down. I wanted to ask your father something.'

Lex turned back to Daisy. 'They're on half-term holiday, as you've probably gathered, and they're on their way out.'

Chloe gave a scornful snort and, catching hold of her sister's hand, said, 'Come on, Imo, let's go and find Mrs Sutton. Dad obviously hasn't got time for us.' She directed a withering stare Daisy's way and then disappeared.

'I do apologise for my daughter.

Chloe especially is proving a bit of a handful these days.' Lex sighed. 'I'm almost at my wits' end if you want the truth.'

'Can't your wife help?' Daisy quietly asked. 'Or maybe you could employ someone to take care of them?' She only just stopped herself from adding, 'You can afford it, after all.'

'Huh, as if. I've been reliably informed they're too old to require the ministrations of a nanny. Come on, let's go into my study. It's increasingly my sanctuary as well as my workplace. I've even thought about fixing a bolt inside the door to ensure total privacy.' He smiled wearily as he turned to lead the way.

Daisy followed him into a large wood-panelled room which, taking into account the floor-to-ceiling shelves of books lining two of the walls, suggested that it also doubled as a library. There was a desk and a high-backed leather office chair, and a massive inglenook fireplace in which a log fire burned. A laptop sat on the desk as well as a phone. Apart from a couple of button-backed wing armchairs sitting each side of the fireplace, that was all. It was immaculately tidy.

Daisy felt a pang of envy. Tidiness was something that constantly eluded her. It had been one of the things that Grant had frequently complained about. 'For God's sake, can't you tidy the place up? You have little else to do all day,' he'd say. Which had been totally untrue, and very unfair. She was always busy. It took a considerable amount of time to look after a house the size of theirs. It hadn't been as large as Pencarrow Hall, but with its five bedrooms and three bathrooms, huge kitchen, breakfast room, dining room, and snug, as well as a larger sitting room, it had still been a very substantial property. She'd had a cleaning lady, Judy, who came in two days a week. She hadn't wanted that, but Grant had insisted on it. 'We must keep up appearances,' he'd insisted. Daisy had been tempted to ask why, but then thought better of it. Grant possessed quite a temper and he hated being challenged by anyone, especially by her. Still, despite what he thought, there had been a great deal for Daisy to do.

'Please sit down.' Lex indicated one of the two armchairs. She did as he asked, and he took the other one, which ensured he was sitting facing her. 'Now, what did you want to ask me?' He smiled beguilingly at her.

A drift of some very expensive aftershave reached her. She felt her breath catch in her throat. Whatever his faults, the man had charisma by the bucketful. And here she was, about to plead for a favour. She couldn't; she simply couldn't do it.

'I shouldn't have come. I'm sorry for wasting your time.' She made as if to get to her feet.

Lex, too, stood up. 'Daisy, please tell me. How can I help? I'm not an ogre. You don't have to look so nervous. Is this because of Chloe? You shouldn't take any notice. She's the same with any woman who comes within a foot of me.'

The look in his eyes urged her to speak. Mustering her rapidly vanishing courage, she took a deep breath and said, 'I went to see the estate agent a few days ago, and — and . . . '

'Go on. And?'

'I need . . . well, I want a dog, and . . . '

'A dog? I don't have any dogs.' A frown tugged at his brow.

'No, no, it's not that. He said the owner of Blue Haven has a no-pets policy.'

'Ye-es, so?' His eyes had narrowed as he continued to stare at her.

'Well, Leah . . . '

'Leah?' He was by this time looking thoroughly confused.

'The artist — you met her in the Ship the other night.'

'Okay. Go on.'

'Well, she told me you know the owner, and I-I was wondering if you could put in a word on my behalf.'

'Why on earth do you want a dog?'

'Well, it's very lonely out there at Sandy Cove, and-and a dog would be company.' She couldn't reveal the real reason she wanted one — that she was frightened. He'd be bound to ask why, and how could she tell him about the blackmail that she was being subjected to? If she did that, she'd have to explain the whole situation, and for all she knew he could very well be the person responsible. He was one of the people she'd come into contact with, after all. Though in all honesty, she couldn't imagine him being foolish enough to have invested in such a scheme. He sounded far too financially astute for that, especially to have made the sort of fortune he had. But she supposed it could be a friend who'd done so and lost all their money, or even a member of his own family.

'It would also give me a reason to walk two or three times a day,' Daisy said. 'It would keep me fit and slim.'

Amusement glittered on Lex's face as

his gaze skimmed her, lingering on her body-hugging T-shirt and the swell of her breasts beneath, then moving to the gentle curve of her hip (she'd made the mistake of removing her jacket). 'You look fit to me. Very fit, in fact,' he murmured throatily. He was making no attempt to hide his appreciation of what he was seeing.

Daisy felt the heat of a blush creeping up her face. Dammit, why couldn't she learn to control it? He'd noticed, of course. How could he not have? Her face was probably scarlet by this time.

He said nothing, though, apart from, 'Okay, I'll see what I can do.' However, his subsequent grin was a knowing one. He was fully aware of how he was affecting her. And why wouldn't he be? He was probably only too accustomed to women throwing themselves at him, and as a result knew exactly how to react to them.

'Thank you so much.' For the second time, she started to get to her feet.

'There's no rush, is there? Stay and

have a cup of coffee. I can get Mrs Sutton to make us a pot.'

'Hasn't she taken the girls some-where?'

'Oh, yes. Well, never mind. I'm pretty handy with the cafetiere.'

But the mere thought of sitting and sharing coffee with Lex Harper in the intimacy of his home was enough to propel Daisy to her feet. 'No, really. It's very kind of you, but I must go. I-I have things to do.'

He looked at her, his scepticism at her excuse only too evident. She tightened her lips. He was too knowing; too confident by half. Either that, or he could read minds, as she'd already suspected once before. 'Will you give me a call when you've had a word with your friend?' she asked him. She then reeled off her mobile number, as well as her email address.

Lex strode to his desk and pulled a notepad from a drawer. 'Write all that down, will you?'

'You probably know the landline

number,' she added.

'I can soon find it if I don't.'

He hadn't really answered her question, she belatedly realised. Which made her wonder — could the night-time caller have been him? 'Good,' she said. 'So, I'll say goodbye.' She proffered her hand.

He took it and held on to it, his gaze a direct one. 'Was that Ben Penter I saw walking you back the other evening?' he asked her.

'Yes. He was a little concerned about my safety, apparently, and he caught up with me.' She didn't say she'd seen Lex watching them. He might want to know why she hadn't acknowledged his wave.

He was still holding her hand, even though she'd tried to tug it away. 'You want to be careful. He's got a bit of an unsavoury reputation.'

'Unsavoury? In what way? He seemed nice enough to me.'

'A reputation with women. He has lots of them, to put it bluntly.'

'As have you, or so I've heard.' She

bit her bottom lip. What the hell was she doing, blurting that out? And there she'd been, thinking she'd learnt to control that particular tendency. What made it worse was that she'd just asked him for his help. Why would he agree if she'd been rude to him? Her and her wretched tongue. If she wasn't careful, she'd be letting slip her real name, and she dreaded to think what might happen then.

As it was, there was a dangerous look to him. His eyes had narrowed to slits. Oh, good grief. What sort of retaliation might he be considering in response to her foolish words? Sadly, her fear seemed set to materialise when he harshly demanded, 'Well, don't stop there. Please — I'm all ears; go on.'

Her apprehension, already acute, only intensified when his fingers tightened painfully over hers. She winced. 'Sorry, that was inexcusable.'

'No, tell me. What have you heard about me? I'd really like to know.'

'Th-that you have a few women

friends, that's all.'

'Well, that's true, I do, but that's all they are — friends. I'm very particular about who I strike up a relationship with, and at the moment there's no one special in my life. That's not to say there couldn't be, of course.' Unexpectedly, he was looking amused now, rather than dangerous.

Relief flooded Daisy. 'I rather think Chloe might take issue with that.'

'Oh, I think I'd manage to pacify Chloe.'

'Are you sure about that? She struck me as being a very single-minded, determined young lady.'

'I'm positive. All I have to do is threaten to cut off her allowance.' He grinned broadly at her.

She couldn't stop herself from grinning back. 'Well, good luck with that.' She hesitated, but then something compelled her to ask, 'So who was the woman with you at the Ship? Andrea, wasn't it?'

This time when she tried to free her

hand he let her, though a disturbing little gleam danced in his eye. 'Andrea's a friend. Her husband is away a lot, so we meet up now and again for a meal, but that's it. Now, is there anything else?' He lifted a quizzical eyebrow at her.

'I'm sorry; I shouldn't have asked. It's none of my business what you do in your private life.'

'No? That's disappointing. I was hoping it might be.'

What the hell did that mean? This man was proving a total enigma. One minute he was provocatively flirtatious, the next cool and standoffish — dangerous, even; then flirtatious once more. A chameleon went through fewer changes, she imagined. He'd be a nightmare to live with. Was that why his wife had left him for another man — a man who would be easier to live with; more predictable?

'But again, watch yourself with Ben. You're a lovely young woman, and he's a normal, red-blooded male.' Lex paused and then went on, his voice seductively throaty, 'As I am. So you shouldn't be surprised if we every so often give way to our baser instincts.'

It was his turn now to proffer his hand. Trembling slightly, she took it.

'Don't look so worried.' This time his squeeze of her fingers was a gentle one, as was his smile. 'You haven't completely blotted your copybook. I'll have a word with Jeff — that's who owns your cottage. You're right, I'm good friends with both him and his wife, Stella. I'm sure he'll let you have your pet. His rule chiefly applies to short summer lets. You're a different case altogether.'

'Thank you. You don't know how much it will mean to me.'

He eyed her for a long moment before asking, 'Enough to persuade you to come out to dinner with me one evening?' His heavy lids shuttered eyes that had briefly glinted with emotion — emotion that looked remarkably like desire.

'Possibly,' she murmured, peeking up at him from beneath her own lowered lids. If she had but known it, it was a highly provocative gesture, and one which Lex took full notice of. He gave a low chuckle and bent his head towards hers.

Daisy froze. Oh God, he was going to kiss her! Was that the price she was expected to pay for his help?

6

But evidently such behaviour would be far too crass for a man of Lex's expertise with women, because all he did was brush Daisy's cheek with his lips. She didn't know whether to feel relieved or disappointed, but then was utterly mortified to discover disappointment was the overriding emotion.

'I'll be in touch, Daisy.' He paused before saying, 'That's a surprisingly old-fashioned name. Whose choice was it, your mother's or father's?'

Not knowing what to make of the sudden turn in the conversation, she glanced up at him. 'Um ... do you know, I've no idea.' She could hardly tell him it had been her own choice. He'd be bound to ask why she'd selected her own name.

Thoroughly disconcerted by that unexpected kiss, as fleeting as it had been, she descended the steps and walked to her car. She was acutely aware of Lex watching her every move, his expression tantalisingly inscrutable as she settled herself in the driver's seat and quickly pulled away.

* * *

Daisy devoted the rest of the morning to searching on the internet for the nearest animal rescue centre. She quickly found one and went onto the website. There were pictures of the dogs that they wished to rehome and she picked one that looked perfect. All she needed now was for Lex to let her know the result of his appeal on her behalf.

When two days had passed with no word from him, her optimism began to diminish. As she'd feared, she'd obviously upset him sufficiently with her unguarded remarks to make him loath to approach his friend, despite his reassurances to the contrary. Surprise was her dominant emotion upon that conclusion. She hadn't expected him to be so petty. He'd seemed to genuinely want to help her.

It was in the early hours of the third day that she was awoken by the sounds of breaking glass somewhere downstairs. Initially she lay paralysed by fear, her thoughts racing through her head. Was someone actually breaking in this time? The person who'd been threatening her? Was he — or she, as unlikely as that seemed — here to harm her? To demand money with menace?

She lifted her mobile phone off the bedside table, preparing to call the police. But what good would that do? There was no police station in Pencarrow; she hadn't as much as glimpsed a policeman or woman since she'd arrived. And anyway, by the time anyone got there she could already be dead in her bed. No, as scared as she was, it was up to her to do something.

In the aftermath of the anonymous letter and then the mysterious phone calls, she'd searched the house and discovered an old cricket bat in a downstairs cupboard. As a precaution, she'd brought it upstairs and placed it on the floor by her bed. It was solidly made and fairly weighty, so it would be as good a weapon as anything.

Quietly now, she climbed out of bed and slipped on her dressing gown. Picking up the bat, she crept noiselessly towards the door and then the landing. With a heart that was hammering so loudly she thought the intruder, if there was indeed one, must surely be able to hear it, she began to descend the stairs slowly, pausing on every third step to listen for the sounds of anyone inside the house.

When she heard nothing — apart from the wind, which had arisen and was rustling the branches of the trees and bushes near the cottage, and the sound of the waves pounding on the sand — she felt brave enough to descend to the hallway and open the door into the kitchen, fully prepared to use the cricket bat if it should prove necessary. The kitchen over-looked the road, and as small as the window was, it did seem the most likely way in for an intruder.

The room, mercifully, was empty, but she saw straightaway that the glass of the window was smashed. It was also swinging open, caught by the wind to bang back and forth in the frame. She looked around then for the smallest sign of someone having been inside, but there was nothing. She strode across the room and closed the window, fastening the catch securely once more.

Had she left it open, allowing a gust of wind to catch it and bang it hard enough to break the glass? Or had someone smashed the glass and then reached inside to open it? She frowned as she struggled to recall her move-ments before going to bed. She'd made a mug of hot chocolate, and although the window had been open earlier she was sure it had been closed by then. She glanced down to the floor. It was covered with shards of glass, as was the table top. Surely if the wind had broken it, most of the glass would be outside. Seeing it all on the inside suggested that someone from outside had inflicted the damage.

Gingerly, Daisy began to pick up the pieces from the floor, and it was then that she saw, lying amongst the shards, a large stone. She lifted it and placed it on the table top. It hadn't got there on its own. Someone had used it to smash the glass. And there were plenty of stones and pebbles littered around the beach; it would have been the work of minutes to find a suitable one. The window was chest-high, so it wouldn't have been difficult to break, especially as it hadn't been double-glazed like the rest of the windows in the house.

One question arose then. Why hadn't the person responsible climbed inside? A possible answer immediately presented itself. Because whoever it was just wanted to frighten her, not harm her. Or maybe the perpetrator had heard her moving around and had run off, which could mean that she was in danger, as he just hadn't had the time to carry out whatever it was he had intended.

She shivered. This made it all the more imperative that she get a dog. It was also important to notify the police. She couldn't let this incident go unreported.

Despite it being the middle of the night, she called 999 and told the person on the other end of the phone what had happened. Amazingly, a couple of policemen were soon ringing her doorbell. She led them into the kitchen and showed them what had happened. She didn't mention the phone calls or the note, however. They studied the stone before one of them, who introduced himself as Officer Tregoran, asked, 'Have you touched it?'

'Only with a piece of kitchen roll,' she answered.

'Good. We'll take it with us and have it tested for fingerprints. You never know, we might have the culprit on record somewhere if he's a known criminal. But if it's just a one-off opportunist thief,' he added with a shrug, 'he probably won't be known to us. Is anything missing?'

'No, I don't think he actually got inside. I must have disturbed him. I heard the glass break, you see, and came down.'

'Okay,' Tregoran said, 'you need to be careful about confronting someone yourself.'

'I know, but I had this.' She showed them the cricket bat.

They both grinned and Tregoran said, 'Okay. Any more trouble, let us know.' And with that, they left.

Daisy felt too hyped up to return to bed, so instead she resorted to her usual panacea in times of trouble: she made a pot of tea and took it into the sitting room to drink. There were still embers glowing in the log-burner from the fire she'd lit earlier in the evening. As she was still shivering — the result, she suspected, of the shock she'd received — she opened the air vents and added another log, and within minutes the flames were burning fiercely, radiating a comforting warmth into the room.

She'd covered the broken window with a flattened cardboard box that she'd found in one of the many cupboards the cottage contained. They were proving to be veritable treasure troves of useful items. Deciding that she'd get the window repaired first thing in the morning, she reached for her laptop and switched it on. It took only a couple of minutes to find the details of a local glazier, and as soon as nine o'clock came round she could telephone him.

This she did, and within another hour he arrived. The job was done quickly and with admirable efficiency. 'Left the window open, did you?' he asked. 'There was a good ol' wind last night. That's probably what did it.'

'Yes.' But Daisy was pretty sure she hadn't left it open. In fact, she was convinced this was another attempt by her blackmailer to frighten her into repaying the stolen money. If only whoever-it-was knew that there was absolutely no chance of it happening, not with her limited funds.

★ ★ ★

An hour later, Lex appeared at her door. 'Oh,' she exclaimed, 'it's you.'

'Yeah, it's me. I thought I'd come in person rather than phone or email you.'

'Come in, then.' She led the way into the small kitchen. 'Coffee? I was just about to make some.'

But he didn't seem to be listening. Instead, he was staring at the newly repaired window. She hadn't got round to cleaning off the putty smears and fingerprints that the glazier had left behind. Despite that, she wouldn't have expected him to notice — unless he was the one responsible for the breakage. Her heart raced. And if he was, here she was offering him coffee.

'Is that fresh glass?'

'Yes. It got broken last night.'

'Did you leave it open? It was very windy.'

'No, I'd closed it. Someone smashed it with a stone.'

He swivelled his head so that he could look at her. 'What?'

'Someone smashed it.'

'Yes, yes, I heard you.'

So why pretend he hadn't? Suspicion once again arose within her.

'Did they get inside?' Belatedly, he appeared concerned; a deep frown tugged at his brow.

Her suspicion of a moment ago now turned itself on its head. Would he be so bothered about it if he had been the culprit? Yes, she mused, if he wished to dispel any suspicion she might have that he was the one responsible.

'No, luckily I heard it and came downstairs.'

He looked horrified. 'You came downstairs? Wasn't that a little foolish?'

By this time she didn't know what to think. His concern could all be an act, of course. 'What was I supposed to do? Wait for him to get in?'

'You should have stayed upstairs and phoned the police.'

'Right, and waited Lord knows how long for them to get here. I could have been attacked or anything.'

'You could have been attacked when you came downstairs.' He did look genuinely shocked. 'Are you okay?'

'A bit shaken, but other than that, fine.' She stared at him, deciding it was time to get down to his reason for being there. She presumed he *had* a reason. Maybe he'd just wanted to see how she'd reacted to the broken window. Whether it had accomplished what he wanted it to: frighten her — no, *terrify* her into paying up. But he could just have phoned her; he didn't need to actually visit.

'Did you have a word with your friend?' she asked him.

'Yes, that's why I'm here. It's okay for you to have a dog, and I can see now why you'd want one.' He paused. 'Has something like this happened before?' He indicated the freshly repaired window. 'Is that why you're so keen?'

She hesitated. 'No — I've just become a bit nervous, that's all. It's lonely out here, and with these long, dark evenings . . . ' She shrugged. 'Well, it would be a comfort to have a dog.'

He eyed her, his expression now one of speculation. 'Ye-es,' he drawled, 'I can see it would be. Is that all that's happened? The broken window?'

For a split second, she was tempted to tell him about the other incidents. But if she did that, and it wasn't him behind them, he'd surely want to know why she was being targeted like this. But then again, if it was him, he'd know anyway. Her thoughts were swirling chaotically. One thing she was sure of: if she went on like this she'd go crazy. But in whom could she put her trust? That was the question.

'Thank you so much for putting in a word for me,' she told him. 'I'm really grateful. I'm planning to get in touch with an animal rescue centre that I've found on the internet.'

'There might not be any need for that. Jeff himself has a dog he needs to find a good home for. He and Stella both work full-time, and he feels it isn't fair to Ollie to be left alone so long.'

'Ollie?'

'Yeah. Short for Oliver. He's of mixed breed. Jeff's not sure exactly what breeds, but he thinks there's a bit of Dobermann in him. In any case, he's assured me he's an excellent guard dog.' He eyed her. 'He's three years old, and fully house-trained, of course.'

'He sounds perfect.'

'Good.' Lex smiled. 'I'll take you to see him, then.'

'What, now?'

'Yeah, if that's convenient for you. Jeff's taking the morning off especially.'

'Great. Just give me a couple of minutes to make sure everything's locked up and secure, and we'll go.'

She ran around the cottage fastening windows, closing doors, and finally locking the front door before she joined Lex outside. He drove what looked like a brand-new black Range Rover, and was already sitting in the driving seat. 'Hop in,' he called as he impatiently toed the accelerator.

Within minutes, they were leaving Pencarrow behind and were on their way to St. Austell. Jeff and his wife lived just outside, on the Truro road.

A man who Daisy assumed was Jeff opened the door of the large double-fronted house that Lex took her to. 'Hi,' he said, holding out a hand and smiling warmly as he did so. 'Please, come in.'

Daisy followed him and Lex inside, and was immediately ambushed by a medium-sized honey-coloured dog. Large chocolate-brown patches liberally freckled his coat. But what particularly struck Daisy were the soulful eyes that he turned upon her. She was enchanted and fell instantly in love.

'Aren't you gorgeous?' She crouched down before him and began to stroke and fondle him. The dog whined and wriggled in ecstasy, his tail energetically swinging from side to side.

'Well,' Jeff said with a grin, 'that's one concern eased. He likes you. So . . . ' His glance at her was an anxious one. 'How about it, Daisy? Will you take him? He's very obedient — well, most of the time.' He grinned again.

'Oh, yes, please. He's exactly what I want.'

'Okay, well, have a week's trial. See how you get on together.'

'That sounds wonderful. I'm sure there won't be a problem.'

And that was that. Job done. She had her dog. A feeling of deep happiness engulfed her. When they returned to the car, Ollie promptly leapt onto the back seat, curled up, and went to sleep.

'Right,' Daisy said, 'I need to get some dog food and another bed, one for upstairs in my bedroom.'

Jeff had given her a few of the basic requirements, saying he wouldn't be needing them anymore, so she didn't have to worry about a collar and lead, or food and water bowls. He'd also given her Ollie's bed and his toys. 'They'll make him feel at home if he's got a few familiar things around him,' he'd said.

Now Daisy asked Lex, 'Where can I go for those?'

'There's a pet shop on our way back.'

★   ★   ★

Within an hour, Lex was dropping her home. He glanced briefly back at Ollie, but spoke to Daisy. 'Are you going to be all right?'

'We'll be fine — won't we, Ollie?'

'Okay. Come on, then. I'll give you a hand with his things.'

'Thanks.'

It didn't take long with two of them, and soon Ollie was eagerly exploring his new home.

'Okay, I must go,' Lex said. 'I've got an appointment I really can't miss.'

'Thank you so much,' Daisy said. 'You've gone way beyond the call of duty. I'm really grateful.'

He cocked his head and, with a disconcertingly gleaming gaze, eyed her. 'How grateful? Grateful enough to have dinner with me later?'

Her heart missed a beat, and her voice quivered as she said, 'Oh — we-ell, I think it's a bit soon to leave Ollie alone. Maybe next week?'

'Sure. I'll be in touch then. If you need anything in the meantime, don't be afraid to ask. Or if you're scared, just pick up the phone.'

'I've got Ollie now, so . . . '

'Hmmm. Well, in the event of another broken window, and if Ollie's no good as a watchdog, call me. I can be here in minutes. Certainly faster than the police will be.'

'Thank you. I appreciate that.' And she really did. His offer was extremely generous and completely unexpected. It was also immensely reassuring. There was no way, she decided, her black-mailer could be him. He'd never have gone to the trouble of finding her a guard dog if it was. He'd want her alone and vulnerable — wouldn't he? Of course, it could just be a clever ploy: reassure her, make her feel safe and protected, and then, out of the blue, attack . . .

'Right. Well then, I'll bid you goodbye,' Lex said, and with that he leant towards her, clearly intending to kiss her — on her cheek? Or on her mouth? Whichever it would have been, she'd never know, because the second he got near her there was a low, menacing growl. They both looked down to see Ollie standing very close to Lex's leg, his hackles raised and his teeth definitely bared.

Lex gave a snort of laughter. 'Well, he's definitely a guard dog. So, with the unattractive prospect of an attack on my leg if I get any closer to you, I'll limit myself to a handshake.'

Once he'd gone, Daisy ladled some food into one of the bowls and watched her new pet hungrily devour it. She sighed with contentment. Already she felt a whole lot safer. In which case, he could sleep in her bedroom. She'd bought him another bed; he might as well make use of it. And just knowing he was at her side would make her feel safer.

'Okay, how about a walk?' she asked once he'd finished eating. 'We could explore the path up to the headland. I haven't ventured up there yet.'

Ollie gave a bark of what she interpreted as approval and ran to the front door. She grinned. This was going to be wonderful. Exercise for them both.

★   ★   ★

The climb up the extremely rough and steep pathway was a tiring one, but the view that met their gazes when they got there made the exertion well worthwhile. Daisy could see all the way to Pencarrow, to the town quay where a lot of people were milling around; she could also look along the creek that ran off the main river. And then there was

Polcurno. Though considerably smaller than Pencarrow, it was also bustling with people. She sat on a conveniently placed wooden bench, Ollie at her feet, and watched the many yachts criss-crossing below her, their sails billowing as they caught the wind.

Perfect. She sighed. Or it would be, if she could just discover who was behind the attempts to blackmail her.

7

The next morning Daisy took Ollie with her into Pencarrow, where the first person she encountered was Freya. She was holding a magnificent bouquet of bronze and yellow chrysanthemums.

'Hi, and who's this?' She looked down at Ollie.

'My new friend and pet, Ollie,' Daisy told her. 'I only got him yesterday.'

Freya glanced back at her. 'Are you allowed to have a dog at the cottage? My understanding is there's usually a strict no-pet policy on holiday rentals.'

'There is, but I persuaded Lex to intervene on my behalf. He's a close friend of the owner.'

A shadow crossed Freya's face at the mere mention of Lex. 'Well, lucky you,' she snapped. 'You certainly don't waste any time, do you?'

'What do you mean?'

'Well, you roll up out of the blue, and within a matter of days you've got the two best-looking men in the town at your beck and call. You'll have to tell me how you do it sometime. It's becoming increasingly evident I need a lesson or two.'

Daisy stared at her, taken aback at the sharpness of her tone as well as her ill-tempered scowl. Where had the friendly woman she'd first encountered gone? 'Well, obviously you mean Lex, but who's the other one?'

'Ben, of course. Look at the way he raced off after you the other evening. You've ensnared him.'

'Ensnared him?' Daisy scoffed. 'You sound like someone from the nine-teenth century.' When Freya looked less than amused by her quip, she decided she'd better try to make amends. 'There's nothing going on with either of them, I can assure you.'

'Really?' Freya clearly didn't believe her.

'Really. They've both been kind,

that's all.' Then, in an attempt to defuse what was rapidly turning into a thoroughly acrimonious exchange, she said, 'Lovely flowers.'

'Yeah. They're to put on my gran's grave. She died a month ago.'

'Oh Freya, I'm so sorry. Were you close to her?'

'Well, as she virtually brought me up, yes, very. My parents always had more important business to attend to than a rather plain and not-very-bright daughter.' She paused, maybe deciding she'd said enough, before bitterly going on. 'Anyway, she killed herself. Jumped off the headland, not far from where you are. Died on the rocks below. Some bastard swindled her out of all her money and then ran off with it.'

Daisy stared at her, aghast. 'Oh my God.'

'Yeah, my words exactly. It was a complete scam. You invest all your money to make huge profits almost immediately. Only, of course, she didn't. Instead, she lost everything — her entire life savings.

She was destitute. She wouldn't ask for help — too proud — so she took the only way out, in her view, that she could.' Tears glistened in Freya's eyes; she dashed them away.

Daisy was speechless. A terrible suspicion was forming within her. Oh no. Not Grant's scheme? Please — no.

'He lived up in your neck of the woods. Grant Carter — have you heard of him? He's disappeared, of course. Caught out several people here. One of them's your neighbour, Johnnie Larson. He's virtually bankrupt too. There's talk he might even have to sell his house. Then there's Lex's father. He lost a huge amount. He's not bankrupt, but still, Lex is very bitter about it. Word got round because one of the earlier investors here did actually get a lot of money back, and of course people rushed to get in on it in the certainty of receiving a large windfall. Totally misguided, sadly.' She pulled a face. 'So, as you can imagine, he's detested by a lot of people in this town — me included.'

Daisy felt the blood draining from her face. So her blackmailer, as she'd already speculated, was almost certainly a local person; and if they themselves hadn't lost a lot of money, they were in all likelihood related to — or at least were close to — someone who had. Dear God, what had she done? She'd run away from one place only to end up in another where several people had been defrauded. What if the person who'd recognised her did actually speak out? She'd most likely be hounded out of town — again.

Freya was staring at her. She must have noticed her deep dismay. 'Oh, good Lord, not you too?'

Daisy nodded. It wasn't a complete lie, because Grant had duped and defrauded her as well, just not in quite the same way that the people here had been. Though she, too had lost practically everything.

'I'm sorry.' Freya seemed to have put aside her bitterness at what she viewed as Daisy's conquest of the two most eligible men in town. For now, at any rate. Daisy wondered then whether Freya was viewing the two of them as partners in misfortune. Her expression was certainly one of sympathy.

'Thanks,' Daisy muttered. She felt terrible; every bit as much of a fraud as Grant had been. Maybe she should come clean and admit Grant was her husband. But would the people here, in contrast to everyone in her home town, believe she'd had no part in it; that she'd been every bit as deceived as they'd been? She couldn't do it, she simply couldn't; she didn't have the courage.

Maybe she should just return to Formby and face up to it all there. To the hostility, the resentment, the unmitigated hatred. Because the truth was, if her identity was revealed here, she'd face exactly the same condemnation. In fact, it had already started.

'So is that why you came here?'

Daisy nodded.

'But what are you living on?'

'I made some money selling what I could of the contents of my house. It's not much, but it'll last until I find a job.' With every word Daisy uttered, her duplicity felt worse and worse. 'Look, I must go, Freya.'

'Okay.' Freya was still looking at her oddly. She hadn't guessed, had she? No, she couldn't have. Why would she? Yet still Daisy's stomach heaved with dread as she waited for Freya to speak.

But all Freya said was, 'We're all going to the pub again this evening. Want to come? I'm sure Ben will be there.' Her tone was gentler now, with only a trace of sarcasm. She lifted a quizzical eyebrow at Daisy. 'He'd probably walk you home again; he's obviously deeply smitten.'

Despite her softened mood, it was transparently clear that Freya was jealous, which did go some way to explaining her bitterness whenever Ben or Lex's name was mentioned. If only Freya knew that Daisy had no intention of getting involved with any man. How could she?

She was still married to Grant. And as she had no idea where he might be, divorce was a very long way off. It would be several years, at least, before he could be declared missing and proceedings could begin.

'I won't, if you don't mind,' she told Freya. 'I don't want to leave Ollie alone just yet. He's not really settled in.'

Heaven knew what Freya would say if she knew that Lex, too, had invited her out, and she'd used exactly the same excuse.

* * *

That night, Daisy went to bed feeling protected and safe. Ollie settled in his own bed on the floor at her side and within minutes was asleep. She smiled to herself and closed her own eyes.

The increasingly familiar calls of the seagulls awoke her the next morning; that and Ollie softly padding across the bedroom, heading for the open door and the stairs down. She squinted at the clock on the bedside table. Eight o'clock.

She sprang out of bed, mainly because Ollie had raced off down the stairs and was now impatiently whining at the front door. Grabbing the tracksuit she'd laid out ready on the nearby chair, she swiftly scrambled into it and followed her pet down.

'Right,' she laughed, 'I can see we're in a hurry.' She clipped on his lead and opened the front door. Ollie immediately dragged her outside to scamper up the road to a grass verge, where he proceeded to relieve himself. 'Good boy,' she praised him, using a small plastic bag that she'd remembered at the last minute to bring with her to clear up behind him. She laughed again as he once more dragged her back to the cottage.

* * *

The remainder of the week passed uneventfully. Daisy and Ollie spent hours roaming together, providing her with the opportunity to become acquainted

142

not just with the area, but also with many of the townspeople. They now called 'Hello' when they saw her, followed up by a friendly and seemingly genuinely meant 'How are you?' They'd then stop and stroke Ollie before proceeding on their way once more. She was beginning to feel a valued part of the community, despite her certainty that someone here knew who she really was.

This feeling of belonging was enhanced when she popped into the gallery one day and Leah asked, 'How do you fancy joining the local drama group? We're always on the lookout for new people. Especially now, when we're about to begin rehearsals for a play. It's a regular event in the town hall. We put one on every New Year. It lightens the bleak January days and gives people something to look forward to.'

'Oh, I don't know. I can't act for the life of me.' But was that strictly true nowadays? She was, after all, permanently acting a part, and pretty effectively too, if she said so herself.

'You could do something else. Help with the costumes.'

'I don't sew.'

'Okay, how are you with a paint-brush? You could give us a hand with the scenery.'

'I'd like that. What's the play?'

'Totally predictable. Well, almost. It's our take on *A Christmas Carol*, with Scrooge becoming Esmerelda Scrooge, a right grumpy old woman, and Tiny Tim changing into Tiny Tina. My eight-year-old niece is going to take that part, though I'll be rehearsing with her at home; her home to begin with. She loves to act, she informs me. I would imagine she'll be very good,' she drily added. 'She certainly acts up at home, so I can guarantee she's had plenty of practice. And it appears she's always wanted to try walking with crutches.' She grinned. 'Anyway, we always have a laugh. Look, come along next Thursday evening — that's our first rehearsal, at six thirty. Well, it's an initial read-through, strictly speaking. Just sit and watch and give us a hand when and if needed. Not that there's much to do at the beginning. It's towards opening night that it all gets frantic.'

'Who else goes?' Daisy asked her.

'Freya. Ben, when his fishing allows him the time. Your neighbour, Johnnie Larson. Have you met him yet? He's a nice guy. Terrific actor, too. He should be a professional, we tell him. Sandra, his wife, doesn't come. Not her scene.'

'I haven't met him yet, but I'd like to.' Oh, good Lord, were half the participants going to turn out to be victims of Grant? She'd have to watch everything she said. As if she wasn't already under enough strain. She gnawed at her bottom lip. Maybe it wasn't such a great idea to join.

'There's a couple of dozen of us altogether,' Leah said. 'Some of them you'll have met, some you won't. It'll give you the opportunity to make some new friends.'

Eventually, albeit reluctantly, Daisy was persuaded to give it a go. 'Okay, I'll come. But don't expect great things.'

'Oh, I wouldn't dream of it.' Leah beamed at her. 'See you then, okay?'

* * *

Before Thursday came round, Lex rang her. 'Hi. How's Ollie? All settled in?'

'Yes,' Daisy told him. 'He's great. We've had some wonderful walks.'

'So how about dinner tonight? A new bistro has opened in St Austell. It's had some good reviews. I thought we could try it.'

Daisy had forgotten all about his promise to ring her and fix a date. 'Oh, um . . . ' She didn't know if she wanted to spend a whole evening in Lex's company, just the two of them. What on earth would they talk about? They had absolutely nothing in common. Yet for all her reservations, there was no mistaking the quickening of her heart-beat; no denying that she was becoming increasingly attracted to him.

'Is there a problem?' he coolly asked.

She could picture his frown of displeasure and the tightening of his mouth. He couldn't be accustomed to women turning him down.

'Well, no, not really.' She eyed Ollie sitting at her feet. He was watching her intently, as if he sensed her dilemma. He gave a whine and began to fidget.

'I'll reserve a table then, shall I?' he pressed her.

Oh, to hell with it. Why not? It had been a long time since such a handsome man had invited her out. Why shouldn't she accept? And why couldn't they simply be friends? There didn't have to be anything more, did there? But remembering the provocative gleam that would occasionally appear in Lex's eye when he regarded her, she wasn't at all sure of that. Nonetheless, she heard herself saying, 'Okay. What time?'

'I'll pick you up at seven.'

'I can drive myself.'

'Certainly not. When I take a woman out I go the whole hog. Fetch her and return her.'

She laughed. 'Okay. I'll be ready then. Um, is it a dressy place?'

'Haven't a clue. Smart casual, I should think. But whatever you wear, I'm sure you'll look stunning.'

Daisy held the phone out in front of her and regarded it as if it was an alien being and not a harmless piece of plastic. He was flirting with her, and not for the first time. She recalled their previous encounters, when he'd made no attempt to hide his physical attraction to her. In fact, he'd made it transparently clear; embarrassingly so a couple of times. She sighed. After nine years of marriage to a man who'd grown increasingly indifferent to her, she was sadly out of practice in the art of responding to the admiration of a man — any man, never mind one as handsome and charismatic as Lex Harper. It wouldn't do, though, to forget that she was still a married woman. Maybe she should tell Lex that. It could ensure that their relationship remained platonic — although she wasn't entirely convinced about that, not when she considered his rather dubious reputation. And if she did tell him, mightn't he want more details? Which would inevitably lead to more lies on her part. She felt she'd already told more than enough of those as it was.

Something else occurred to her then. Now that she knew about his father's financial losses, it seemed all the more reason to suspect that it could be Lex behind everything that was happening to her. So was she recklessly agreeing to spend the evening with her blackmailer?

* * *

The question was one that occupied Daisy's thoughts for the better part of the rest of the morning. She even found herself confiding her anxiety to Ollie at one point. 'What should I do? Should I cancel? But supposing he isn't the person behind everything? I'd be denying myself a pleasant evening out for no good reason.'

The dog promptly sat down and regarded her, head to one side, before he gave a couple of barks.

'You think I should go? Or are you telling me not to?' She frowned. Ollie whined and wriggled his bottom. 'Which is it? Oh, I wish you could talk.' She then snorted at her own foolishness. Honestly, was she really asking a dog for advice? Was this what she'd descended to?

'Come on, then. Let's go for a walk before it starts to get dark, and I can have a think about it.'

Yet again, she headed up to the headland and its ruined castle. It had become her favourite destination. Whatever the weather, she would perch on the bench, umbrella up if it was raining, Ollie at her feet, and absorb the panoramic view while she pondered whatever problem was concerning her at the time. The occasional person walked past, but apart from a friendly 'Hello' they left her alone with her thoughts.

But today, a familiar voice hailed her. 'Hi. I was on my way to see you and saw you heading up here. Do you mind if I join you?'

It was Ben. Ollie sat more upright at Daisy's side and gave a low, menacing growl.

'Ssh, Ollie. He's a friend.' She stroked his head before glancing back at Ben, her expression a quizzical one.

'I was expecting to see you at the pub sometime.' He looked at Ollie. 'I guess he's the reason for your absence.'

Daisy smiled and glanced back down at her dog, gently tugging at one of his silky-soft ears. 'Yes, I wanted him to be settled before I left him alone.' Ollie whined as if in perfect agreement with that sentiment. Daisy's smile broadened.

'What made you decide to have a dog?' Ben didn't look particularly pleased about that. Daisy uneasily wondered why. She didn't want to believe that Ben was her blackmailer. And why would he be? She hadn't heard that he'd lost any money to Grant's scheme; and if he had, knowing how effective the rumour mill was here in Pencarrow, she surely would have done.

'Bit of a tie, aren't they?' he went on.

'A bit, I suppose, but I don't mind, and he's great company with the evenings getting darker and darker.'

'Oh, well, if it's company you want, I do a very nice sideline in that particular occupation.' He appeared to have put his displeasure to one side as he waggled his eyebrows at her.

She laughed, reassured by his tomfoolery. 'I'm sure you do. And I expect you've had plenty of practice.'

'Well, some.' And he, too, laughed. 'Actually, I was wondering — would you like to come out with me this evening? We could have a bite to eat. As long as he's not coming, of course.' He swept his glance towards Ollie. 'He could put a bit of a dampener on things.'

'Oh, I'm sorry. I'm already committed this evening.'

A frown tugged at his brow. 'Committed? Who to?'

'Lex Harper rang me earlier and asked me to go with him to a new bistro in St Austell that he's keen to try.'

Ben pulled a face, part wry and part

scornful. 'You're taking the risk of going out with him, are you? In spite of my warning?'

Daisy didn't answer. He'd obviously presumed that she was discounting his warning about Lex and his ruthlessness. However, she didn't feel she had to justify her actions to him — or anyone else.

'Well,' he went on, clearly interpreting her silence for what it was — a hint that he should mind his own business, 'I can't compete with that, I'm afraid. From what I've heard, it's fine dining, which means the prices are way out of my league. In fact, nowadays, with the state my finances are in, I'd probably need to get a second mortgage. I was thinking more of a fish-and-chip supper at the Ship.' He shrugged as if he wasn't that bothered by her refusal, but something in his expression — an odd little glint in his eye — told Daisy he was actually very bothered.

'Maybe another time? I'll see you on Thursday, in any case,' she told him, hoping that it would go some way to appeasing him. 'I've been invited along to the drama group's first read-through with a view to helping out backstage.'

'Oh?' His expression of hopeful optimism reminded her of Ollie's when she offered either a walk or food. 'I'll see you then. I can't always get there, but this week I'm free. So are you heading back? Rain's forecast in a bit. You don't want to get caught out up here in it.'

'I might go a little further. If I exhaust Ollie, he'll sleep all evening while I'm out.'

'Fine. See you on Thursday.' And without saying any more, Ben turned round and left.

Daisy stared after him, gnawing at her bottom lip with her teeth, reflecting on what he'd said: he'd need a second mortgage nowadays, given the state of his finances, to take her out to somewhere like the bistro. Did that mean he had lost money to Grant's fraud, too?

Oh God. She groaned softly. For the

first time in years she had two highly attractive men pursuing her, and the danger was that one of them could be her blackmailer.

8

It took Daisy a long time to decide what to wear that evening. From what Ben had said, the bistro was an inordinately expensive place for fine dining, so the women at least would most likely be dressed to the nines. In the end, with time fast running out, she plumped for one of the few designer garments she'd kept. It had been her favourite, which was why she'd been loath to get rid of it. Now she thanked heaven she hadn't.

It was a dark blue dress, sleeveless, and speckled with tiny pale-blue and pink rosebuds. The silky fabric gently hugged the lines of her figure without being too obvious about it, and the crossover bodice sported a V-neckline that was moderately low-cut and revealed just the tops of her full breasts, as well as the merest hint of a shadowy cleavage. The fitted skirt finished at her knees.

She teamed it with a blue shrug and a pair of matching high-heeled blue shoes. A small clutch bag completed the ensemble.

She then considered her reflection. The colour brought out the deep blue of her eyes, but was it too dressy? 'What do you think, Ollie?'

The dog barked once and then whined pitifully, clearly sensing her imminent departure. She crouched down in front of him. He was stretched out on the floor, his head propped on his two front paws as he gazed beseechingly up at her.

'I won't be long, darling. You have a nice sleep.'

As if he understood, he went to his bed in the sitting room. As he settled himself down, the doorbell rang.

'There's my date.' How strange it felt to be saying that. Her date. Anyone would think she was eighteen instead of thirty. It certainly felt that way, if the energetic pounding of her heart was anything to go by. She was on her way to the door when her mobile phone rang. She checked the screen and saw that it was her mother calling.

'Mum, can I ring you back? I'm just on my way out.'

'Are you? Well, that's good. Where are you going?'

'Out with a friend.'

'Male or female?'

'As it happens, it's male.' The bell rang again, this time for longer. 'Look, I really do have to go. He's here. I'll call you later.'

She opened the door and there was Lex, looking impossibly handsome in an immaculately tailored dark tan jacket. This he had teamed with a pair of trousers that were a shade paler, and a dark brown open-necked shirt. With a heartbeat that was threatening to go into hyperdrive, Daisy slid her arms into the jacket she'd always worn with this particular dress, at the same time noting the way his gaze slid over her.

'You look gorgeous,' he said with a lazy smile. 'Ready?'

'Yes.' Feeling girlishly shy now, as

well as nervous about how the evening would pan out, Daisy camouflaged her blushes by devoting all her attention to pulling the door closed behind her before spending a couple more moments thoroughly checking it was actually shut. When she turned, it was to find Lex's gaze still on her, slightly quizzical now. Neither of them noticed the figure lurking in the shadows at the start of the path up to the headland. A substantial bush effectively concealed whoever it was from view without restricting the onlooker's gaze.

* ★ ★

The road they took was practically empty of traffic, so it didn't take long to reach the bistro. One look as they walked inside told Daisy she'd made the right choice of outfit. The women, as she'd anticipated, were glamorously dressed, and each and every one of them swept their gazes Lex and Daisy's way. Mind you, their eyes didn't linger on Daisy; to a woman, they all turned their attention to Lex. He, however, looked oblivious to the silent but obvious admiration. A whisper of relief passed through Daisy. If it had been Grant with her, he would have returned their looks with unabashed interest, humiliating her as he'd had a habit of doing during the last few years of their marriage. It had been no wonder that she had, more and more, felt she failed to live up to his expectations.

The conversation throughout the journey had been pretty general; mundane, even. Lex had said nothing to alarm Daisy or make her fear he might be trying to force his attentions on her. In fact, his first question had been to ask if Ollie was settling in okay.

She'd replied, 'Very well. He's a great companion, almost seeming to talk back to me.' She snorted with amusement. 'In fact, I spend a good deal of my day asking his advice.'

Lex grinned. 'And does he give it?'

'Do you know, in a way he does. Just

asking the question sometimes leads to the answer. Foolish, aren't I?'

'Not really. Don't they say a dog is man's best friend? Well, in this case, a woman's.'

'I thought you said you didn't have any dogs?'

'Until recently, I've been forced to travel far too often on business. I didn't consider it fair to ask the household staff to look after an animal.'

Household staff? How many did he have, for goodness sake?

'But apart from that, Annie, my wife, or Annabel as she insists on being called nowadays, wasn't particularly fond of them.' He shrugged, drawing Daisy's gaze to the breadth of his shoulders beneath his tailored jacket. She'd make a bet that somewhere in that huge house of his there was a gym, and from the look of him, he made regular and very effective use of it.

'How about Chloe and Imogen? Wouldn't they like a pet? Most children do.'

'Imogen would. Chloe's not too keen, like her mother. Ah, we've arrived.' And that put an end to that particular topic of conversation.

Once they were seated at a small, beautifully laid table for two, Lex ordered a bottle of the restaurant's very best champagne. In response to Daisy's look of query, he simply said, 'We'll celebrate.'

'Celebrate what?'

'Our being out together. I consider it quite an achievement.' He regarded her from beneath lowered eyelids — a way of masking his thoughts, she decided, and a tactic he made regular use of.

'Do you? Why?'

'I wasn't at all sure you'd agree to come.'

Despite his words of reservation, there was something in his tone that contradicted what he'd just said. She'd stake money on the fact that he'd been absolutely confident of her agreement. Irritation with him suffused her.

'Weren't you?' Even she could discern the scepticism in her voice, so he must surely be able to do so. To her surprise, however, he didn't pick up on it. Instead, he tilted his head to one side and, subjecting her to a particularly penetrating stare, asked, 'So how come a woman like you is still single? What are you?'

'What am I? What do you mean?'

'How old are you?'

'That's a rather impertinent question,' she smartly quipped. 'A true gentleman never asks a lady her age.'

He instantly came back with a smooth, 'Maybe I'm not a true gentleman.' He then arched an eyebrow at her, sending Daisy's heart rate into the sort of hyperdrive she'd felt threatened with earlier. She frowned. Oh, good Lord, why had she agreed to come out with such a man; a man who would actually admit to not being a gentleman? Somewhat belatedly, and far too late to do anything about it, she conceded that she didn't feel at all safe with him. So she was inordinately relieved when the waiter arrived and distracted him by pouring their champagne.

Sadly, that distraction didn't last long. 'Well, let me see,' Lex drawled, his gaze once more riveting itself on Daisy, 'I'd guess mid- to late twenties. If you're here alone, there's obviously not a man in your life.'

'I'm thirty, and I have been married,' she blurted.

Once again, he raised an eyebrow. It clearly was something he was fond of doing whenever he wished his displeasure to be felt by whoever was with him. But all he said was, 'Oh?'

'I'm, uh, separated.'

The brow snapped back down as his eyes narrowed and darkened. As she'd witnessed once before, he looked alarmingly dangerous. Daisy quivered with unease. Lex Harper, she suspected, would make a pretty formidable adversary, and one that she had no desire to take on. For the second time in as many minutes, she bitterly regretted having agreed to come out with him. Well, it would be the last time.

His tone was a harsh one as he said, 'You told me the first time we met that you weren't married. And now suddenly you say you're separated.' The eyes that had been dark just seconds ago now lightened into deadly chips of ice. 'Are you planning to get divorced any time soon?'

She chose not to answer that, whether out of caution or fear she couldn't have said. In any case, it was none of his business whether she was married or not. She decided it was time to move the conversation away from the topic of her private life. 'You're divorced, aren't you? At least, that's what you told me.'

'Yes, it was finalised six months ago. You didn't answer my question.' His tone had in no way softened. 'Are you planning on getting divorced?'

She looked away from his level gaze and began to toy with the stem of her champagne glass. His tenaciousness had her comparing him with a terrier about to devour his favourite bone. It didn't help that the bone in question seemed to be her. 'Yes, eventually.'

'What's the problem? Why can't you start proceedings now? I mean, you're already separated. What's stopping you?'

She stared back at him, anger gradually replacing the trepidation. Again she asked herself why he couldn't mind his own damned business. What was it to him whether she was married, divorced, or separated? But more to the point, why on earth had she told him she was married? For the umpteenth time, she asked herself why she didn't stop and think before she opened her mouth. Now, just as she'd feared, he was asking all sorts of difficult questions. Questions she couldn't truthfully answer.

Supposing he told other people she was married? She could already hear Freya's questions — accusations, even — of deceit, and Lord knew what else. She'd told Freya she'd just come out of a difficult relationship, so she hadn't altogether lied, just bent the truth a little. Not that admitting it made Daisy feel any better. And then there were Ben and Leah. She'd led each of them to believe she was single. They'd all want to know why.

She closed her eyes briefly as despair engulfed her. What had she done? Why hadn't she simply told everyone in the first place that she was married but separated? Nobody would have thought anything of it, not nowadays. But now . . . well, now they'd all ask questions. Unanswerable questions.

As if to fulfil that expectation, Lex immediately demanded, 'Where is he? Is that the problem? Is he out of touch?'

'You could say that. He's . . . abroad, and moves round a lot.'

'Is that why you're here, in a rented cottage, alone? Are you hiding from him?'

Oh, good Lord. Now what should she say? He'd hit the nail on the head. She was indeed hiding, just not from Grant. 'Um — I needed to get away, to clear my head.'

But Lex clearly wasn't going to let

the subject rest. 'Have you heard from him at all?'

'Not for a while, no.'

'Excuse me, sir, madam. Are you ready to order your food?'

Daisy let out a long, low sigh of relief. What had she been thinking, to tell Lex all of that? Why hadn't she just remained silent? But he must have detected her discomfort, because once they'd both given their order, he took pity on her and changed the subject.

'What did you do before you were married? Or did you continue to work afterwards?'

'I was a PA to the managing director of a firm called Kincaid Engineering, but that was seven or eight years ago. I haven't worked since. But I'll soon be needing a job.' She smiled ruefully at him. 'Part-time, if possible, now that I've got Ollie at home.'

He sat back in his chair and again stared at her, something kindling in his eyes. At least he'd lost that dangerous look. 'I'm looking for a new PA. My last

one had to leave.' He paused. 'Due to
. . . certain problems. Would you be
interested?'

Daisy made no attempt to hide her
surprise at his offer. She'd more than
once thought of several occupations he
might offer her, but not one of them
had been a legitimate job offer. 'Well, I
might be. It would depend on what the
job entailed, obviously. My experience
is in the engineering world.'

'It's nothing complicated. Mainly computer work, dealing with correspondence,
arranging meetings, taking notes, book-
ing hotel rooms, the occasional flight
tickets, that sort of thing. How's your
shorthand?'

'Pretty good, or it was. I'm a bit
rusty, but I'm sure I could soon brush
up on that. How many hours a week
would you want?'

He shrugged, once again drawing her
gaze to the breadth of his shoulders. A
quiver of desire pierced her. Desire she
swiftly and rigorously suppressed.

'Twenty or so. You could arrange

them to suit yourself and Ollie, unless I was going somewhere specific and required your note-taking skills. I would pay.' He mentioned an amount that sounded excessively generous to Daisy. It was certainly a lot more than she'd received in her previous job. 'I work mainly from home, especially when the girls are with me.'

The girls! Chloe, in particular. Daisy hadn't given a thought to her. She wouldn't approve. She wondered then if it was Chloe who'd been the 'certain problem' with his last PA. She decided to ask him straight out, weary as she was with pussyfooting around, debating what questions to ask and what remarks she could safely make.

'And how would Chloe view my presence in the house?'

Lex shrugged, as if the question was too trivial to bother about. 'She'd have to put up with it. She's not always there, in any case.'

'Okay . . . Can I have time to think it over?'

'Sure. Now, more champagne?'

'Why not?'

He topped up her glass and asked, 'Tell me about yourself. Any siblings?'

'One brother.'

'And you have no children, clearly.'

'No. I would have liked some, but it just didn't happen.'

'And your parents, where are they?'

This was beginning to feel like an interrogation, she irritably decided. 'Liverpool.' She'd better stick to the story she'd already told Freya.

'You're a long way away from them.'

'Yes. As I said, I needed a break.'

'From what? Not your husband, presumably?'

Daisy swallowed nervously. Were there no questions this man wouldn't ask? No boundaries he wouldn't attempt to stray beyond? Again, the need to remain on her guard forcibly struck her, because it was becoming increasingly evident that Lex Harper missed nothing.

'Life in general, I suppose. I wanted some peace and quiet.' Once again she was acutely aware of having said too much. Supposing he asked, 'Peace and quiet from what?'

However, all he said was, 'Well, you've got that at Blue Haven all right.' His stare was again a penetrating one. Had he sensed she wasn't being quite truthful? 'I find it all a little strange.'

For the second time in as many minutes, she swallowed nervously. Here it came — more questions, as she'd expected. 'You do?'

'Yes. Here you are, an attractive woman — well, a beautiful woman, if I'm honest. And yet you've opted to spend your time living alone in a Cornish backwater. Surely you want more than that?'

'Why would I? I'm getting to know a lot of people locally. I'm going to be joining the drama society.'

'Are you an actress, then?'

'No, but there's lots of action taking place backstage apparently.'

He didn't say anything for a moment, but just stared at her. Then he drawled,

'I believe Ben Penter's involved. Is he the attraction? Is it with him that the backstage action will take place?'

'I wasn't talking about that sort of action,' she indignantly protested.

'Then what sort of action were you talking about?' His gaze clashed with hers, his expression shuttered and impenetrable. He was proving an exceedingly difficult man to read. It was maddening. She liked to know where she stood with people, and she was miles away from that with this man.

'I-I'm helping out with painting the scenery, things like that.'

'Are you sure that's all? He's obviously interested in you.'

'Well, people could say the same thing about you. If they knew you'd invited me out . . . ' She met his gaze defiantly. What would he have to say to that?

To her annoyance, he looked completely unfazed. 'And they'd be right,' he smoothly said.

'We're friends, that's all,' she strenuously insisted.

'Who? You and me, or you and Ben?'

'Well both, I suppose. Though frankly, I barely know either of you.'

'Well, I would argue about me being included in that verdict. I think we've got to know each other pretty well.'

He looked hurt and Daisy felt a pang of guilt. After all, he had taken her to get Ollie and then helped her buy all the things she needed for her new pet. Maybe she should retract her statement, or at least elaborate on what she'd meant, which was that their relationship hadn't progressed to anything more intimate than friendship. That wasn't to say she hadn't greatly valued his help in introducing her to Jeff and Ollie.

Before she could do so, however, he went on, 'Does Ben know you believe you barely know him?' He was watching her intently.

'I've no idea.'

'Has he asked you out?'

'Yes, but I said I was seeing you this evening.'

He didn't speak for a long moment.

Then, 'Are you going to go out with him?'

'Why are you so interested?' His questions were beginning to feel like an intrusion.

'I'd have thought that was obvious. I'm attracted to you.' She stared at him. He grinned. 'That's shocked you?'

'It has, yes.'

'Why?'

'Well, you were with another woman the other evening, so I thought — assumed . . .'

He waited for her to go on. When she didn't, he asked, 'You thought — assumed . . . ?'

She decided to disregard his gentle mockery. 'I assumed that the two of you were involved.'

'Well, we're not. As I told you when you visited me, we were just two friends enjoying a drink and a meal. Her husband was away.'

'Right.'

'Don't you believe me?'

She shrugged. She wasn't sure she

did. An extremely handsome man and a very attractive woman out for the evening together — it did look suspicious. All she said, though, was, 'If you say that's all it was, who am I to argue with you?'

Again, his gaze was an intense one. She waited for whatever was coming next. 'Are you interested in me?'

'How can I be? I'm still married.' She marvelled at the composed way she'd answered him. How had she managed that when her heart was thumping fit to burst from her chest at the bluntness of his question?

'But eventually, and before too long, I hope you won't be.'

And to that she had no answer. Because until she knew where Grant was, she was tied to him, at least for the foreseeable future.

'Daisy?'

'I have no idea where he is. He left me two months ago; and with no contact between us, how can I begin divorce proceedings?'

9

In the wake of that blunt declaration, Lex, for once, looked lost for words. 'Well,' he finally said, 'you do have a problem. But even so, I need you to know I still want you, divorced or not. And he has left you, so in my book that means you're free to do as you want and see who you want.'

It was Daisy's turn now to be shocked into silence. The last thing she'd expected was for him to be quite so explicit about his intentions towards her.

By the time they left the bistro, conversation had returned to normal — to Daisy's immeasurable relief — and they talked easily and amicably all the way back to Blue Haven. Lex told her he had an older brother who'd emigrated ten years previously to Canada. His parents, however, lived just a couple of miles away. He smiled fondly. 'I see a lot of them.'

The time passed quickly and they reached Blue Haven in record time. Once there, and despite the fact that it had started to drizzle quite heavily, Lex insisted on seeing Daisy to the door. Ollie, alert as ever to any extraneous noises, was standing just inside, and he was barking loudly.

'Do you want to come in for a coffee or a nightcap?' Daisy politely asked, mainly because she felt she should. He had, after all, been a generous and interesting escort.

He eyed her from beneath heavy eyelids. 'Better not. Things might get a little out of hand if I'm completely alone in there with you.'

Daisy felt her cheeks warming at the significance of those words.

'And Ollie sounds as if he might have a go at me. I'm hoping his bark is worse than his bite.' He grinned before murmuring, 'In case I decide to risk crossing the threshold one of these evenings.' He slipped an arm around her and said a husky, 'Goodnight, Daisy,' before muttering, 'Sorry, but I really have to do this.' And he slid his fingers through her hair as he lowered his head, capturing her lips with his.

The kiss that followed paralysed Daisy with its sheer passion. She'd never been kissed in such a way before, not even by Grant. Her lips parted involuntarily beneath the pressure of his tongue as her body fell against his, moulding itself to him, as if they'd been made to be in each other's arms. With a throaty groan, he pulled her closer, thus ensuring she became acutely aware of his physical arousal. She simply couldn't help herself then; her hands slid up his chest and around the back of his neck, and her fingers, in turn, slid in amongst the strands of his hair. As if in direct response to this, his hand lowered, cupping her buttock, pulling her even harder against him as he again groaned, almost in anguish this time, 'Oh God.' Then, just as suddenly as he'd begun to kiss her, he roughly thrust her away.

'You'd better go in before I do something I shouldn't,' he muttered.

'What? Out here?' she teasingly asked. 'In the rain?'

He grinned shakily. 'Yes, out here, and in the rain.'

'Okay, point taken,' she smartly riposted. 'Goodnight then.'

'Daisy, I want to see you again.' Heavy lids had lowered over eyes that were smouldering. She could almost physically feel the heat of the passion that was emanating from him.

'Oh, I'm sure you will. After all, we do live in the same small town.' It was her turn then to grin.

'Watch it,' he growled, before boldly threatening, 'or I might have to take you in hand.'

'I thought you'd already done that,' she softly said. After which, she quickly opened the door and nipped inside. Once there, she stood still, her back pressed against the wood, her heartbeat thunderous as she considered what had just happened. Surely he wouldn't have kissed her so passionately if he was the one threatening her. Or would he? It could be a well-thought-out tactic to allay any suspicions she might be starting to have about him.

Eventually she went to bed. She'd taken Ollie out for a last walk, but he hadn't seemed to want to go far before returning to the house. And she couldn't blame him. The drizzle had turned into a steady rainfall, heavy enough to soak everything around them. Branches dripped beads of moisture to form puddles on the road. It all conspired to ensure she didn't notice the figure still standing well back in the shadows, peering intently through the dense curtain of gloom at her.

★ ★ ★

Half an hour later Daisy was still lying awake, the evening's events churning chaotically in her head. She didn't know what to make of Lex's lovemaking; didn't want to believe it could all have been part of a cold-blooded and well-executed plan to lull her into trusting him, while all the while he was trying to scare and blackmail her.

The landline phone rang down in the hallway, startling her, its tone shrill in the utter quiet of the night. 'Oh, damn,' she muttered, 'I forgot to ring Mum.' She had to answer. Her mother would simply keep ringing until she did. She was a real worry wart. Though why she didn't ring her daughter's mobile phone, Daisy didn't know, as she always kept that at her side.

She squinted at the bedside clock. Eleven thirty. Her mother would expect her to still be up; Daisy had never been an early-to-bed person. She made her way down the stairs, Ollie close behind her, then lifted the receiver to her ear.

'Hi, Mum. Sorry.'

A muffled voice asked, 'Did you think I didn't mean it? You'd better believe me when I say I do. I will expose your identity if you don't contact a newspaper and promise to repay all the money you stole. You have my word on that — bitch.'

The line went dead. Daisy stared at the receiver in horror. What the hell was she supposed to do? The caller must know she couldn't repay anything. If whoever it was knew who she was, and where she was, as they obviously did, surely they'd see she had no money? For God's sake, she was living in a small rented cottage and drove a cheap second-hand car. It was glaringly obvious that she barely had a penny to her name, let alone several million pounds. A person would have to be an idiot to believe she'd choose to live this way, if in reality she had access to so much wealth.

With a hand that shook, she replaced the receiver. Maybe the blackmailer *was* fully aware she had no money, in which case their intention must be to simply frighten her. So what did that mean? That they were exacting some sort of revenge; a form of punishment — if she couldn't pay the money back, she'd be forced to pay by living her life in fear of some sort of physical retribution?

She began to tremble. Could whoever it was be outside, waiting to see what she'd do? It seemed a reasonable supposition. They knew she was at home; she'd answered the phone. She ran into the kitchen and peered through the window to the road beyond. The rain had stopped, she could see, but the sky remained heavy with cloud, which meant there was no moon or stars; nothing to illuminate anyone standing out there. Nevertheless, she directed her gaze along the road, both towards the town and then in the direction of the footpath that led up to the headland. At first, as she'd expected, she could see nothing; but then something stirred in the shadows and a figure stepped forward. A figure that was cloaked in some sort of voluminous garment with a hood that was pulled up and forward, thereby shielding the person's face.

Anger powerful enough to banish any fear had Daisy opening the window.

'Who are you?' she shouted. 'Show yourself. You don't frighten me.'

The person didn't answer, other than with a scornful-sounding snort. And then whoever it was swung, broke into a run, and swiftly disappeared in the direction of the town.

It must have been the person who'd made the phone call. No one else would have a reason to skulk outside on a night like this. Daisy ran back into the hall, intending to phone the police. But what would be the point? Whoever it had been would be long gone by the time they arrived. And as the phone the caller had used had most likely been a pay-as-you-go mobile, they wouldn't be able to trace it anyway.

Slowly she climbed back up the stairs, Ollie still hugging her heels. 'Oh Ollie, what am I going to do? If my identity is made public, I'll be ostracised; hounded out of town, in all probability — at least by the people who've lost their money.'

And that list included Lex's father.

What on earth would Lex say if he found out who she was? She'd lied over and over again to him. Unless — could the person out there have been him? He knew she was in; he'd brought her home. Could he have parked his car outside his hotel and walked back? It was perfectly possible.

She slowed her step as she reached the top of the stairs. It hadn't looked like Lex. Though it had been dark, she had been able to make out that the figure wasn't tall enough to be him; and despite the large coat, she'd also detected that the build had been wrong. She couldn't be one hundred percent sure of that, however. But in spite of what she'd thought earlier, it didn't seem Lex's way of doing things, to stand silently in the dark. He was so forthright. He'd have accused her in person, wouldn't he? Not threatened from the shadows.

★   ★   ★

When Thursday evening arrived, Daisy seriously considered not going to the first rehearsal of the Christmas play. Yet, she reasoned, if the person watching her happened to be a member of the drama group, she might be able to pick up some sort of clue, a hint as to their identity. Something in their eyes, their tone of voice as they spoke to her, or a hint of malice. She'd also meet her nearest neighbour. What was his name? Oh yes, Johnnie Larson.

After a great deal of shilly-shallying, one minute deciding she would go, the next that she wouldn't, she finally left the house and climbed into her car. One thing she had been completely set on was that she would drive into Pencarrow trusting that she'd find a parking space somewhere. The prospect of having to walk back later alone in the darkness of the night, and possibly in the rain — the weather had seriously deteriorated over the past days, but then it was November — had proved too daunting under the current circumstances. Who knew what was being planned next for her?

However, all didn't go as she'd hoped. A parking space near to the town hall proved impossible to find, and she ended up having to drive to the other side of the town to a car park. She pulled a face. She might as well have walked in the first place. The distance she'd have to go was about the same.

So it was much later than she'd planned before she arrived to join the group. Everyone else appeared to be there. They must have all opted to walk.

Freya was the first to speak. 'You're late. Did you walk?'

'No, I drove, but I've had to park the car in the North Street car park and walk back. I might as well have walked in the first place, but I couldn't face the trek back later, not in the dark.' She gave a wry smile. 'Pathetic, I know.'

'Oh, you needn't have worried about that,' Freya calmly assured her. 'I'm sure Ben would have obliged and gone with you.' The last few words had more than a trace of acid to them, unmistakably conveying the fact that she wasn't as untroubled by the prospect as she made out.

Daisy eyed her. She could never decide whether Freya was joking or genuinely annoyed with her. 'Freya,' she softly murmured, 'I'm not interested in Ben — or anyone else, come to that.'

Freya cocked an eyebrow at her. 'Really? Not even Lex? How come you went out to dinner with him?'

The jungle drums had obviously been working overtime. But even as Daisy had the thought, another considerably more mundane explanation occurred to her. 'Did Ben tell you that?'

'Yeah, and he was pretty cross, I can tell you.'

'It was a one-off.'

Something else occurred to Daisy then. Could the figure in the shadows have been Ben? He'd known she was going out with Lex, and where, so he could have hazarded a pretty accurate guess as to the time of their return. He could then have come to the cottage a bit earlier and waited in the shadows till he saw her and Lex arrive. Once Lex was gone, he could have made the phone call. In which case, he must have recognised Daisy that first evening in the Ship. Had he decided there and then to try and make it look as if he was attracted to her? Was his plan — just as she had wondered about Lex — to get close enough to know of her whereabouts at all times, and then to persecute her?

She frowned and gnawed at her bottom lip. She had to stop being suspicious of everyone. She couldn't live her life afraid to trust anyone, never knowing a moment's peace or security.

'Hey. Glad you came.'

It was Ben. Had her thoughts about him somehow summoned him to her side? She stared at him now, and it was as if she was seeing him for the first time. She hadn't noticed before, not even when he'd walked her home from the pub, but he wasn't a tall man, nowhere near as tall as Lex; maybe five feet eight. He was of a slimmer build too. It could easily have been him she saw outside the cottage. Yet, as she'd reflected once before, she hadn't heard that he'd lost any money to the scam, although he had implied he was short of money. Maybe he hadn't told anyone about his losses, preferring to keep his stupidity to himself.

'Hi,' she said to him. 'I thought I'd see how things work, and if there's anything I can do to help.'

'Have you met Johnnie? Your nearest neighbour.' Ben indicated the man walking just behind him. 'Johnnie, come and meet Daisy. She's renting Blue Haven for the winter.'

'Yes, I think I've seen you going past the house.' Johnnie grinned. 'Brave lady. The wind blows straight off the sea there at certain times. You'll need to batten down the hatches then.'

'Don't you get the same?' she asked.

'Not quite as bad. We're sheltered to a certain extent by the opposite headland, and Polcurno of course.'

Daisy now studied him as he stood

alongside Ben. The two of them were about the same height and build. Her watcher could have been either one of them. There was no way of telling, not unless she'd been able to see the facial features. But then her heartbeat quickened. Johnnie Larson was wearing a dark coat very similar to the one the person last night had been wearing. And he had lost a lot of money; enough to force him to sell his home, if the gossip was correct. More than enough incentive to try and get some of it back.

'Hey.' Ben waved his hand in front of her face. 'Are you still with us?'

'Oh, sorry, yes. It's nice to meet you, Mr Larson.' She held out her hand to him.

He took it, smiling. 'Oh, please, it's Johnnie. We don't stand on ceremony in these parts. Maybe it's different where you come from. The north somewhere, isn't it?'

'Yes, Lancashire. Liverpool, actually.'

'A bit of a change for you then. How are you liking it here?'

He was watching her closely now; too closely. Daisy was beginning to feel a tad uneasy. In fact, his stare was starting to feel intrusive, as if he was trying to see right inside her. Or — her heart skipped a beat — as if he'd recognised her. But if that had only just happened, it would mean it couldn't have been him outside the cottage. Everything seemed to be pointing to Ben. Or had Johnnie seen her passing his house and recognised her? Living as close to her as he did would make it very easy to get to her cottage and then make his escape to his own house again, without anyone seeing him. Oh God, she was going to go crazy if she kept sizing up everybody she met for the role of blackmailer. But she simply couldn't help herself.

Somehow she managed to reply to Johnnie's question, even if her voice did quiver slightly. 'Very much. I used to holiday here as a child.'

'Yes, Ben said.'

'Daisy,' Freya said, tugging at her

arm, 'we're about to begin the read-through.'

'Okay.'

'Actually, you couldn't read the part of Mrs Cratchit, could you? Jane, who was taking that role, couldn't make it.'

'Well, I'll tell you now I'm no actress, but I'll do my best.'

As it turned out, she did it very well. It helped that she'd read the book at least a couple of times, and had also seen a film of it.

'Hey,' Ben called to her, 'you're a natural. Leah,' he called across the hall to the other woman. She'd got up to go and make tea for everyone. 'You should cast Daisy as Ma Cratchit.'

'Do you know,' she called back, 'I've been thinking the same thing. It's beginning to look as if Jane can't find the time to do it; her mother's been taken ill. So it would work well.'

'Oh no,' Daisy instantly protested. 'Really, I couldn't.'

Leah returned, bearing a tray filled with mugs of tea. 'Yes, you could. It's not a very big part — a half a dozen lines, that's all — so you could still help out with the scenery. You were great.'

'Was I?'

'Yeah, you were a complete professional,' Ben said.

Freya said nothing. She didn't need to. Her resentful glare in Daisy's direction spoke for her.

A sense of defiance filled Daisy. Why shouldn't she do it? It would give her the opportunity to get to know people better, and provide a much-needed distraction from all that was happening to her. And it really wasn't Daisy's fault that Freya was so insecure; so evidently jealous of her and her friendships with Lex and Ben.

'Okay, I'll do it.'

10

Once that was settled, the conversation veered off in another direction entirely, to that of the costumes and how much of what they already had could be re-used with just a few modifications.

Freya, who was to play Esmerelda Scrooge, imperiously demanded a new costume, saying that there was nothing remotely suitable for her role; but other than that she didn't say much at all. Daisy was beginning to feel as if Freya's bad mood was somehow all her fault. But she couldn't help it if Ben had taken a liking to her. Or Lex. She'd done nothing to actively encourage either of them, though Ben had once or twice that evening flirted outrageously with her and, despite her lingering suspicion of him, she had found herself light-heartedly responding. He was playing the part of Bob Cratchit and had used every opportunity available to him to slip his arm around her. Each time, she'd been acutely aware of Freya's dark and disapproving glance.

It was a great relief when eventually Freya recovered her good humour and even murmured to Daisy at the end of the evening, 'Are you going to be okay walking back to your car on your own?'

'Good Lord, yes. It's not that far,' she lied.

'I'm sure someone would walk with you.'

Did she mean Ben? But Daisy was swiftly disabused of that notion, because Freya went on, 'I'm sure Johnnie would go with you. You could give him a lift home then, because he walked here.'

'Oh no,' Daisy hurriedly said. The last person she wanted walking with her was him. She didn't know the man, and it could well be him tormenting her. 'I'll be fine, really. I wouldn't want to bother him.'

She then quickly said her goodbyes, retrieved her jacket from the cloakroom and left the hall, keen to return to her car and get home. She set off with every appearance of confidence, and all was well to start with because the street was well-lit. She walked past the Quayside hotel. Dennis was standing in the doorway smoking a cigarette.

'Hello,' she said. 'How are you?'

'I'm fine,' he responded. 'Aren't you headed the wrong way to get home?'

'Well, yes, but I had to park my car in the North Street car park.' She pulled a face. 'So that's where I'm headed.'

'Will you be okay on your own?' he went on to ask. 'It's quite a walk.'

'I'll be fine. I'm getting used to walking here. It'll only take me five minutes.'

'It might take a bit longer than that. Still — I'll see you again sometime, maybe?'

'I'm sure you will. It's only a small town.' She smiled at him. 'Maybe in the Ship.'

He didn't answer, but threw his cigarette stub down and stood on it, before turning and walking inside.

Daisy continued on along the street. He was a strange one, too. It was then she realised that he hadn't smiled once throughout their entire conversation. Not that it had been a long conversation; but still, a smile wouldn't have hurt him. But then again, he hadn't smiled at the pub either. In fact, he was a bit of a misery all round. He and Freya should suit each other very well. Maybe she'd suggest it to Freya. She chuckled to herself.

Daisy stopped smiling, however, the further away from the town she got. The street lighting abruptly came to an end, leaving the road ahead inky black; so black that she could barely see her hand when she held it up in front of her. Once again, there was no moon to light her way. In fact, the cloud had become so heavy that a thick drizzle had begun to descend, beading her hair and shoulders with moisture.

Instinctively, she quickened her step. She could see now why Dennis had asked if she'd be all right. Perhaps she should have asked him to walk with her. She shivered and thought, *No way.* He was so unsmiling, so creepy. He made her uneasy. She shivered a second time and silently cursed the fact that she hadn't brought a hat with her. She hated her head getting wet, and the fact that it was just seemed to compound her profound unease, especially as there wasn't another soul around. The silence was absolute and eerie. Which was why she so clearly detected what sounded like footsteps somewhere behind her.

She stopped and swivelled her head to peer through the dense curtain of drizzle; not surprisingly, she couldn't see anyone. In fact, she couldn't see for more than a couple of metres. But as the sounds had stopped, she decided it must be her imagination, which was pretty active at the best of times, let alone in circumstances like these. She recalled Dennis again and his unsmiling demeanour. And it belatedly occurred to her that he knew where she lived.

A chill whispered through her as she remembered the manner in which he'd watched her that first evening at the Ship. He'd creeped her out then as well, mainly because his eyes had looked almost opaque and completely expressionless. She'd had no idea what he'd been thinking. And just moments ago she'd told him where she was headed. Was it a coincidence that she'd heard what sounded like footsteps behind her? Despairing tears stung her eyes. She was beginning to feel there was no one she could trust; no one at all.

She turned back and hurried on. For several minutes there was only the noise of her own footsteps, and then she heard what sounded like a piece of gravel being scuffed. Again she glanced back before looking to either side of her. On one side of the road there was a row of houses interspersed with a few shops, all closed at this time of the evening. On the other, there was a high wall behind which lay the car park. For the second time, she stopped walking and turned to peer through the thickening drizzle; a drizzle that was fast turning into rain, as it seemed to have a nasty habit of doing. Once more, she listened carefully, but again could hear nothing.

Was she really imagining things, or could there be someone walking on the other side of the wall keeping pace with her? Dennis? But how would he have got in there? She hadn't noticed another entrance when she'd parked her car. The one she'd walked out through earlier lay a bit further along the road. Could he have climbed over the wall? But wouldn't she have heard him doing that?

Abandoning any show of bravery, and with an imagination that was running riot, she broke into a fast trot, hell-bent on getting back to her car. But supposing he was waiting for her on the other side of the wall; waiting for her to enter the car park? Once inside, she'd be completely out of sight from the road. He would be able to do whatever he wanted. Panic engulfed her then, quickening her heartbeat and making her stomach lurch in fear. She was alone, terrifyingly so. Someone could attack her and there was no one to hear her cries for help.

For the third time she stopped, and for the third time there wasn't a sound to be heard. A lone owl hooted from a row of fir trees just up ahead; they lined the left-hand side of the road where the buildings ended, their shapes taking on a sinister appearance in the darkness. Something loomed on the top of the wall to one side of her. She leapt backwards, a scream rising in her throat. It meowed and jumped down into the road.

Daisy gasped. It was a cat, a bloody cat. She gave a snort of contempt. She'd been terrified by a cat. She laughed and continued walking towards the car park entrance just up ahead. What was happening to her? Her fear was intensifying to such an extent that she was starting to see danger where there was none, suspecting everyone. She had to stop it right now, or in a very short time she'd be a nervous wreck. Yet the phone calls and the broken window had been real, as had the person she'd seen standing in the shadows watching the cottage.

She quickened her pace again, and once she was through the car park entrance she jogged across to her car. She unlocked the door and all but fell inside. After which, she wasted no time in turning on the engine and racing out into the road. She moved so quickly that she failed to spot the person standing in the shadows in front of the wall, back pressed against the brick, grinning at the spectacle of Daisy's ashen face and frightened eyes.

★ ★ ★

Daisy barely slept that night, unable to prevent the memory of recent events filling her head. She told herself over and over that the evening's fright had most probably been an imagined one. But the other incidents hadn't been; they'd been all very real. And then there was the letter. It had been clear. The person who'd written it knew who she was. Someone was terrorising her for their own ends, and she couldn't stop asking herself who.

There were several candidates: Lex, Ben, Johnnie Larson, and now Dennis. Johnnie was the most likely culprit. He was in the perfect position to observe all her comings and goings; she had to walk past his house wherever she went, other than up to the headland. But would anyone go to such lengths? He'd have to take up a more or less permanent position at an upstairs window. Yet he had lost a considerable sum of money, so she supposed he might consider it worthwhile if he managed to get some of it back.

What about Ben and Dennis? Daisy still had no idea whether they had invested in the scheme and lost everything, and she could hardly ask them. If she did, they'd be bound to wonder why. In Ben's case, it could be all that was needed to jog his memory if he'd seen her photograph. Then what was to prevent him telling people?

But most important of all, what about Lex? Was he really capable of inviting Daisy out, flirting with her, and kissing her with such passion, before proceeding to terrorise her?

* * *

Come morning, she was in such an agitated state of mind that the mere ringing of her mobile phone just after eight o'clock had her practically leaping from her chair. Ollie, already highly sensitive to her moods, whined. He'd taken to following her wherever she went in the house, as if afraid to allow her out of his sight.

She picked up the phone and nervously regarded it. So far her night-time caller hadn't rung her mobile or called during the day, but she supposed there was always a first time, and she had given her number to a few people by this time. She pressed the button to answer, but didn't at first say anything.

'Daisy?'

It was Lex. She still didn't know his number to put it into her phone, so it hadn't shown on her screen. Now she wondered who he'd expected to be answering. It was her number he'd rung.

'Yes?' she finally asked. She couldn't quite rid herself of the suspicion that somehow he could be the one behind everything. For the first time, it occurred to her that while it might not actually be him standing in the darkness, it could be someone he was paying to do his dirty work for him. He'd easily be able to afford it — the only one of the suspects who could, she imagined.

'Are you okay?' he asked her.

'I'm fine.'

'You don't sound it.'

'Don't I?'

'No, you sound . . . tense.'

'Well, it is early.'

'Yes, sorry about that, but I wanted to catch you before you went out anywhere.'

'What can I do for you?'

'Do you really want me to tell you

that?' His voice was low and husky, but she could hear that he was grinning.

'Maybe not,' she tartly replied.

'That's a bit disappointing, but not entirely unexpected.'

She said nothing. She wasn't in the mood for any of his flirting.

'I was wondering,' he went on, 'have you thought any more about my job offer? You'd work here at the house. I have an office, so you wouldn't have to do much in the way of commuting.'

Oh good Lord, she'd completely forgotten about that, what with everything else that was happening to her. She was tempted to agree. It would give her something else to think about; something to do. But could she trust him? Yet, hard-headed logic suggested that if he was the one responsible, he'd hardly have offered her a job. And why would he have enabled her to get a dog? It didn't make sense, if he wanted her to be alone and frightened.

'Um — I haven't had much time.'

'Really? What have you been up to?'

His tone had cooled. He didn't believe her. He thought she was making excuses.

'All sorts. I think I told you I've joined the drama group. I've been persuaded to play the part of Mrs Cratchit.'

She heard his snort of disbelief quite clearly. Her hackles rose. Didn't he think she could act?

'Wasn't she a meek and mild little person? Do you think you'll manage to come across as that?'

She ignored that gibe. 'It's only a small part. And no, she's not at all meek and mild. Far from it. She more than stands up for herself and her family.'

'I see. The role should suit you down to the ground then. There'll be very little acting needing to be done.' Again he sounded amused.

'What does that remark mean?'

'Well, you have no trouble speaking your mind.'

'Believe me, there are quite a lot of things I'm tempted to say but don't.' She almost added, 'Especially where you're concerned.' Instead she concentrated on suppressing her mounting irritation with him. She mutely vowed she'd show him she could act a part. And she'd do as he asked: she'd act as his assistant, despite her uncertainty about his involvement in what was happening to her.

'Okay,' she said.

'What, you'll do it?'

'Yes.'

'Good.' Lex sounded surprised. He'd expected her to say no. She didn't know what to make of that.

'So when do you want me?' she asked him.

'How about now?' he murmured. The tone of his voice was downright seductive, and she'd have to be an idiot to misunderstand his innuendo.

'I'm talking about the job,' she tightly retaliated.

'So am I,' he smoothly replied. 'What did you think I was talking about?'

The man was impossible. He sounded as if he was interpreting her acceptance of his job offer as an acceptance of a physical relationship with him. She'd have to make the situation very clear right from the start — that she never, ever mixed business with her personal life. The kiss they'd shared would be the first as well as the last, and he'd have to accept that, or how was she going to work with him? Maybe she should rescind her agreement. But she badly needed the money.

'So — when?' she again asked.

'How about Monday? My correspondence is beginning to pile up, and I've got an important business meeting at the end of next week for which I'll need you and your shorthand.'

'Okay. If I start at eleven o'clock and work until three, how does that sound?'

'Perfect. Of course, there will be the odd spot of overtime.'

'Will there?' He hadn't mentioned that. 'How much overtime? I can't leave Ollie for too long. After all, it's why Jeff wanted a new home for him in the first place.'

'It would just be the occasional evening, when I need someone to co-host a business dinner. You could still leave at three and return later.'

'B-but . . . ' She was about to ask, 'Don't you have someone else who could do that? Andrea, say?' but decided against it. Who knew what his answer would be? He'd in all likelihood offer Daisy the job of girlfriend — even mistress — as well. For a suitable remuneration, naturally. She wondered what sort of monetary value he'd place on *that* position.

'Okay,' she said again.

'Monday it is, then. I'll see you at eleven sharp.'

But as Daisy switched her phone off, she was immediately beset by doubts. How on earth was she going to work for the man when she was so powerfully attracted to him? Especially when he had admitted he wanted her too? And who knew what he meant by that. Would it just be for sex, or was he thinking of a more permanent arrangement? And what about Ollie? How was he going to adjust to being left alone for four hours, five days a week?

Still, anything would be better than staying here in the cottage with just a dog for company, even a dog as intelligent as Ollie. She'd still have the evenings to get through, though. She sighed.

'Oh, Ollie, what shall I do? Maybe I should just return to Formby. What do you think? I'd take you with me.' She snorted. There she went again, talking to a dog for goodness sake. How sad was that? 'Come on, let's go for a long walk, eh?' Ollie barked his agreement. 'I'll take that as a yes. There's a lane we haven't explored yet. We'll do that, shall we?'

The morning was an inviting one, the sky an unbroken blue, the previous evening's drizzle vanquished by the bright sunshine. Astonishing weather for November, and utterly perfect for a walk. Daisy took a deep breath, savouring everything from the tang of the sea air to the sight of the last golden leaves still stubbornly clinging to the trees. A blackbird sang joyfully from the top branches of one of them. She smiled, then sniffed. She could smell smoke. A bonfire? She glanced around. She couldn't see any houses, yet there must be one somewhere. Or maybe the smoke was drifting on the breeze from someone's chimney. Johnnie's, maybe? She hadn't lit her own log-burner yet today.

The lane she and Ollie were walking along was such a rough one, it could hardly be described as a lane at all. It was more of a wide footpath with a mixture of sand and soil underfoot. Damp and slightly muddy now from the previous evening's rain, it was edged with verges of grass, dying brambles and bracken, and piles of fallen leaves. Chestnut and oak trees grew up out of this, their trunks interspersed with a tangle of shrubs and bushes, their interwoven branches forming a basic sort of hedgerow. There were gaps amongst them, however, and they revealed glimpses of a turquoise and completely calm sea. Lozenges of sunlight speckled the surface, gleaming like randomly scattered jewels. All of a sudden, the idea of leaving it all was a completely unacceptable one to Daisy, not least because it meant she'd be running away once again. Surely, she asked herself, if she didn't respond to the blackmail, sooner or later her tormentor would grow weary of it? And if he did reveal her identity, well, she'd deal with it.

She let Ollie off the lead now that they were well away from any risk of traffic, and he raced ahead of her, stopping on a frequent basis to sniff amongst the dead leaves and bracken, searching out the intriguing scents of other animals.

They'd been walking for about half an hour when Ollie unexpectedly stopped his explorations and stood perfectly still, his ears erect, his nose pointing straight ahead as he stared towards the nearby bend in the lane. He began to growl deep in his throat. It was a menacing sound, making Daisy stop and stare in the same direction as her pet. What had Ollie seen or heard? In an instant, all the fear and dread of the night before returned. She darted a nervous glance around, but could see no one through the dense foliage that surrounded her.

'Ollie,' she softly called, 'come; come to me.' The dog ignored her and began to bark. 'What is it?' she hissed.

But she could see what it was. Someone was there, standing among the trees. She could just about make out some sort of shape.

'Ollie,' she called, louder this time. Ollie started forward. Daisy began to back away. 'Who's there?' she shouted. 'Show yourself.'

Another dog barked. Ollie started to whine and then wag his tail. At the same time, an elderly man appeared. He was wearing a dark blue anorak. He also had a dog at his side.

'Are you calling me?' he asked in a tremulous voice. He looked almost as scared as she felt.

'Oh, s-sorry,' Daisy began. 'I thought . . .' Her words petered out. What had she thought? That someone was stalking her?

Sneaking up on her? Waiting to assault her? Last evening and the episode with the cat had been bad enough, but now she'd made a fool of herself yet again, this time in front of somebody else. She really had to stop overreacting like this. It was ridiculous.

Ollie had run over to the other dog and the two of them were sniffing at each other, tails wagging in almost perfect unison.

'What?' The elderly man eyed her uncertainly. 'Did you think that I was up to no good?' He smiled then, his pale eyes twinkling with amusement. 'Still, it's understandable. It is a bit solitary along here. You're wise to bring your dog with you.' He was keenly observing her now. 'Are you all right? You look a bit pale.'

'I'm fine. I don't know this lane, and I was a bit unsure when Ollie — my dog — began to bark. I'm a relative newcomer to the town.'

'Oh, are you the young lady who's renting Blue Haven?'

'Yes.'

'I heard you're here on your own — well, apart from your pet. A bit lonely, isn't it?'

'It is, yes. But I'm gradually getting used to it.'

'I live a little further along the road from you, the other side of the Larsons. We're closer to the town. My name's Alec Tomlin.' He held out a hand to her as a broad smile wreathed his face. 'If you ever get too lonely, come and see us. My wife, Belinda, would love to see a fresh face. We're at number forty-seven.'

'Thank you. I might take you up on that. Um — I met Mr Larson last night in the town hall. He's a member of the drama group that I've just joined.'

'Johnnie's a bit . . . well, let's just say he and his wife like to keep themselves to themselves. I was surprised when I heard he'd joined the drama group. It seems to be the only thing he is involved in, mind you. His wife, Sandra, doesn't even do that. I did hear they'd had a bit of bad luck.' He shrugged. 'Whether that's why she keeps herself apart, I don't know. They lost most of their money in some sort of financial scam. Me, I'm always suspicious of any scheme that sounds too good to be true, because it usually is.' He beamed at her again, clearly proud of his good sense.

'Me too,' she quietly said.

'So what do you do, my dear?' He cocked his head to one side. 'Do you work?'

'I'm due to begin a new job on Monday, actually.'

'You're planning to stay with us then?'

'Oh yes, at least for the winter.'

'Where are you from?'

'Liverpool.'

'I know it well. My wife has family up there.' He frowned. 'In fact, the fraud that Larson fell victim to was carried out from near there somewhere. Formby, I believe.'

'Oh.' Daisy smiled weakly. 'Really?'

'Yes, the chap responsible sounded a

real rogue. Him and his wife, according to the papers. Mind you, you can't believe all you read, can you?'

She shook her head, desperately hoping he hadn't seen her photograph, and if he had that he didn't remember it — or her. 'No, you certainly can't.' And who should know that better than her?

'Still, quite a few people here fell for the fraud. One old lady, Lindsay Carne, even killed herself. Terrible story.'

'Yes, I heard.'

'Well, I must get on. It's been a real pleasure talking to you, my dear. Don't forget now. If you ever feel like a bit of company, number forty-seven. We'd really like to see you. Winter here can be a bit of a lonely time.'

She breathed a deep sigh of relief as she watched him walk away. He hadn't remembered her. But as he hadn't lost any money, she supposed he had no reason to. 'What a lovely man,' she said to Ollie as they walked on. 'And you found a new friend, too.'

There she went again, talking to a flippin' animal. She was spending too much time on her own; she needed some company, otherwise she was in very real danger of turning into one of those people who walked around permanently talking to themselves, as well as their dog. She grinned, and suddenly, despite her reservations about him, she was glad that she'd accepted Lex's offer of a job. All she had to do now was somehow fend off his amorous advances while doing it.

'Come on,' she said to Ollie, 'let's run, shall we? I certainly need the exercise.'

It was a full two and a half hours before they arrived back at Blue Haven. Daisy was exhausted, but at the same time exhilarated, and feeling much less stressed into the bargain. She'd walked a good deal further than she'd intended, following a coastal pathway right round to the next small bay, Penkerris, before returning home.

She devoted the rest of that afternoon to sorting out some appropriate clothes for work on Monday. She was determined to begin as she meant to go on: present an efficient and business-like appearance, and hope that Lex got her message loud and clear. There was to be no romantic involvement between them, no matter how he felt about her.

★　★　★

It was Sunday before Daisy's mobile phone rang again. This time it was her mother. She bit her lip. She'd meant to ring her, but with all that had been happening she'd completely forgotten.

'Mum?' Her tone was a cautious one as she waited for the recriminations to start.

'Darcey.'

'It's Daisy, Mum, remember?'

'Oh yes. Sorry, darling. I've been expecting you to call.'

'Sorry, Mum. I've been so busy with one thing and another that it slipped my mind.'

'That's okay. The reason I'm phoning

is, could we come down and stay for a little while? We'd love to see the cottage, and your dad could do with a bit of rest and relaxation. He's been so busy at work; it's been very stressful.'

'Oh.' She hadn't been expecting that. 'Well, I'm actually starting a new job myself tomorrow, as PA to a local businessman. It's only part-time, which will suit me.'

'That was quick, but well done.'

'Yes, and I've also acquired a dog.'

'My word, you have been busy. You're settling in, then?'

'I am, yes.'

'Well, we could walk the dog while you're out. I could also help out on the cooking front.'

It did sound very tempting. 'When do you want to come?'

'Well, how does Tuesday or Wednesday sound?'

'Okay. Make it Wednesday, can you? It'll give me a bit more time to prepare things.' Not least to clear and then clean the guest bedroom, which had become a bit of a dumping place for items she wasn't using at present.

'That's fine.'

'Good. So Dad's okay, is he?'

'He will be. The firm's been taken over and there's talk of redundancies.'

'No.' Daisy was shocked. Her father had worked there for the past twenty-five years. 'Surely he won't be one of them? Not with his record?'

'To be honest, love, we're not sure. But he's due some holiday, so he decided to take it now while he can.'

'Oh, Mum.'

'I know. These past two or three months have been very worrying.'

'But Dad didn't say anything before I left.'

'No, well, he didn't want to worry you. You had enough on your plate as it was, with your own troubles.'

Despite her mother's reassurances, Daisy felt bad. She should have noticed something was wrong. Had it been in the local paper? The trouble was, she'd stopped reading it. The news had been

224

all about her and Grant, and she'd reached a point where she simply couldn't take any more.

'Well, you'll be very welcome here,' she told her mother. 'In fact, it will be great to have you both.'

And it would be. Because whoever was trying to frighten her would surely realise someone was with her and halt their malicious campaign. For good, hopefully.

11

Daisy spent Sunday evening making a start on her planned preparation of the guest bedroom for her parents' stay, her excitement at the prospect of having them there intensifying as she did so. However, that combined with her anxiety about starting her job the next day meant that her sleep was intermittent, which led to her feeling heavy-headed and distinctly jittery the following morning.

Nevertheless, she was dressed and ready by ten thirty in the only suit she had deemed appropriate — a dark grey fitted skirt and jacket. She'd got rid of all of her smarter outfits, having come to the conclusion she'd have no need of them where she was going. She'd also kept a pair of black high-heeled shoes, and she was wearing a cream chemise beneath the jacket. She eyed herself in the mirror. Was the look too severe? She would, after all, be working in some-one's home. Somehow she'd have to fit in a shopping trip; find a couple of alternatives. An outfit that would be smart, but wouldn't look quite so austere.

In an effort to soften the look a little, she undid the two top buttons of the jacket to reveal a couple of inches of cream lace. She then swapped the black shoes for a pair that were a pale grey suede. That was better, she decided. She didn't look as if she was dressed to attend a funeral now.

She'd taken Ollie for an early walk and he was now lying on her bed, watch-ing her with eyes that were full of what looked like despair. She guessed that his animal instincts had told him that some-thing was different about this morning; something bad was about to happen. She leant over him and tenderly fondled his ears. She'd grown to deeply love this dog in the short space of time he'd been with her. In fact, she couldn't imagine life now without him.

'I won't be long,' she softly told him. 'I'll be home again before you know it. I've left you food and water.' Despite this, though, she wasn't at all sure about leaving him. She kissed the top of his head and sighed. Needs must, and she needed to work to provide herself with an income. She simply couldn't afford to turn down Lex's very generous offer. 'The time will soon pass.'

Ollie rested his chin on his forepaws and continued to gaze soulfully up at her, giving a tiny heart-tugging whine as he did so. Somehow Daisy steeled herself to turn away, and picking up her handbag, she headed for the stairs and the front door.

She was almost at the foot of the stairs before she noticed the envelope lying on the doormat. She could see that her name was printed in capital letters on the front and, moreover, that there was no stamp; it had been hand-delivered. When? It hadn't been there when she'd first got up and come downstairs. And she hadn't heard the sound of the letter-box snapping shut either, which she usually did. So it must have been pushed through while she was upstairs dressing.

She bent down and picked it up, hesitating only for a second before ripping the envelope open and reading the words, also printed, on the single sheet of paper inside: THIS IS YOUR LAST WARNING.

That was all. She stared at it for several seconds as anger replaced the heaving sensation of nausea. Its meaning was unmistakable. If she didn't pay up, her identity would be revealed. But what the hell was she supposed to do? She hadn't got the finances to repay people. And who was she supposed to pay the money to? Each individual who'd been so cruelly defrauded? How was she expected to find them?

She stared at the words, hopelessness filling her, her determination to deal with any exposure if and when it happened shot to pieces. Anger suffused her then and she tore the paper into shreds. Maybe she should simply come clean and confess to everyone; tell them who she was, and trust that they'd believe her when she said she'd had no idea what Grant was doing. Surely the people she now considered her friends would believe her?

But there was something not quite right about any of this. A genuine blackmailer would issue instructions about paying and how to do it. So far there'd been nothing of that nature, just these threats to reveal her identity. It made her wonder all over again if this was all about revenge and punishment rather than repaying the lost money.

She made a decision: she'd bide her time and see what happened next before she did something rash, something she could never undo. Yet, supposing her persecutor revealed her name anyway? Which was a very real risk if she failed to respond to the letter. Again she asked herself how she was supposed to respond. There had been no means of communication given, other than instructions to contact a national newspaper saying she wished to repay the stolen money. And that she couldn't bring herself to do. They'd make hay with the story — that was the way of the media — and she'd be splashed all over the front pages again. The situation was an impossible one. She couldn't see any way out. Her shoulders slumped.

The mere idea of having to move once more was unbearable; unthinkable. And where would she go, in any case? The same thing could happen wherever she ended up; someone could recognise her, and that would be that. It had only been three months, after all, since the scam had been exposed.

She checked her wristwatch. Oh good Lord, it was almost eleven. She was going to be late, and on her first morning.

She opened the front door, calling, 'Bye, Ollie,' but the dog didn't appear at the top of the stairs, so she closed the door behind her. He was clearly sulking.

Daisy was almost ten minutes late by
the time she parked her car in front of
the house. She rang the bell and waited.
To her astonishment, Lex himself opened
the door, just as he'd done on her first
visit. She'd expected a housekeeper to
appear. She certainly hadn't anticipated
a man of Lex's wealth and importance
doing it himself.

'S-sorry,' she haltingly said, 'I was
delayed.'

He didn't immediately reply. Instead,
he allowed his eyes to slowly roam all
over her, initially in surprise, but then
with barely veiled amusement.

'Is this some sort of not-so-subtle
warning?' he eventually asked, indicat-
ing the dark suit.

'Warning?'

'Yes, to keep my distance. To maintain
a business-like attitude.' He wasn't making
any attempt now to hide his mirth.

Daisy expected him to laugh out loud
at any moment. And if he did . . . well,

she wouldn't be answerable for her actions. However, she didn't say a word.

'If it is,' he went on huskily, 'I have to tell you it's not a very successful one. In fact, you look gorgeous. Very sexy. I've always loved a woman dressed in dark colours — especially when she doesn't appear to be wearing much more than a touch of lace underneath.'

Daisy stared at him, beyond speech. This was exactly what she'd been afraid of. Quickly, she refastened the jacket buttons that she'd foolishly undone, ignoring the glitter of his eyes. Instead of sending him a signal that she was here to work and not for any other purpose, her choice of clothes had actually encouraged him. Well, she wasn't going to put up with this sort of innuendo. It was unacceptable in a place of work. In fact, it could be described as sexual harassment. And that was illegal.

She glared her outrage at him. It made not a scrap of difference. Instead of being cowed, he gave a deep-throated chuckle. She tightened her lips. He was impossible. There was no way she could do this. 'Do you know,' she said, 'I've changed my mind about the job.' And she swivelled, intending to return immediately to her car and drive away.

'Hey, hey.' He caught hold of her arm, swinging her back to face him again. 'It was a joke.' Tilting his head to one side, he regarded her blazing eyes and flushed face. 'I'm sorry. I was completely out of order. In fact, my words were unacceptable.'

'Yes, they were. And just so there's no further misunderstanding, I make it a strict policy to never, ever mix business with my-my social life.'

He eyed her, momentarily looking unsure of himself. 'Really? Never?'

'Yes. Never.'

'I see.' His expression had reverted to normal at this point, and once again conveyed his complete self-assurance. 'Message understood. I will be entirely proper — whenever you're at work.' He paused, before adding in an undertone,

'Can't promise anything when you're not, however.'

Daisy regarded him from beneath a lowered brow. The man was completely maddening; deliberately provocative. And utterly, utterly irresistible, she concluded as she gazed into his still-gleaming eyes.

Dear God. This wasn't a good idea, generous salary or not. She allowed herself a soft sigh, ignoring the amused quirk at the corners of his mouth. The wretched man could probably mind-read as well, which could lead to all manner of complications. She'd give it a week and see how it went. But if he tried anything untoward, that would be it. She'd be out of here faster than a whippet chasing a hare.

But Daisy's fears proved groundless, because from that moment Lex acted with utter professionalism towards her. He politely ushered her into a small room that was fitted out as an office, and where she'd be presumably working — on her own, judging by the one small desk in the centre of the room.

He obviously conducted his own business in the library that he'd shown her into on her first visit. She ignored the stab of disappointment that that engendered. For some reason, she'd expected to be working alongside him. Why, she didn't know. She'd had her own office in her previous job. And, she firmly chided herself, his presence would have been a serious distraction. No, it was much better this way. She'd get a whole lot more work done, and that was what she was there for, after all.

Lex indicated that she take the seat behind the desk, whereupon he proceeded to list what sounded to Daisy like an inordinately large amount of work for her to do. He couldn't want it all done in a single day, surely?

Her sense of horror must have revealed itself on her face, because he asked, perfectly seriously, 'Do you think you'll be able to cope?'

'Um, well, I don't think I'll manage to complete it all in a day.'

'No?' He arched an expectant and faintly surprised eyebrow at her.

'No,' she firmly said.

He laughed then. 'Don't worry. If it takes a week or more, that's fine. I just wanted you to know what the job entails, that's all. I'm very confident that you'll be extremely efficient.'

Huh. She wished she was. However, once he'd gone and she got down to things, all her past experience and skills returned. Luckily she'd kept abreast of all the latest technological developments, so there were no problems there; and as the day progressed, her confidence in her abilities grew. This, she told herself, was going to be a piece of cake.

The four hours passed swiftly and, before she realised it, it was three o'clock and time to leave. The housekeeper, Donna, had brought her some lunch, which was fortunate because she hadn't thought about bringing any herself. Donna even stayed for a few minutes and chatted. She'd been friendly and good-natured. Just one of her remarks had bothered

Daisy, and that had been when she'd said, 'I don't know how Chloe will react to you being here. Mind you, you'll be gone before she gets home from school, so consider yourself lucky. She made the last woman's life a misery, especially during the school holidays. Not that there's another of those until Christmas.'

Daisy didn't respond, deciding it might be best not to. She didn't know how discreet Donna was, and she didn't want any words of complaint about Lex's oldest daughter filtering back to anyone in the family.

'Chloe's problem is that she thinks every woman's after Lex, even me to start with, and I'm a good ten years older than him.' Donna eyed Daisy then. 'She'll definitely see you as a threat.'

Daisy's spirits spiralled downwards. 'Oh.'

'So be warned. Try and stay out of Madam's way if you can.'

Then something occurred to Daisy. The things that had been happening to her — it couldn't be Chloe behind it all, could it? Trying to drive her away? Maybe it wasn't about the money, as she'd wondered more than once. Maybe she simply wanted Daisy to leave. She could easily have seen Daisy's photograph in the newspaper and, upon recognising her during that first encounter, decided to utilise the situation for her own ends. Or maybe she did genuinely want to get her grandfather's money back for him. But, as Daisy had asked herself several times, how could she achieve that without providing some way for Daisy to pay? And another thing — would Chloe be out at night, alone and wandering about? Would Lex allow that? Or was she sneaking out unbeknownst to her father? Another question presented itself then: how would she get from the house to Daisy's cottage? It was too far to walk.

* * *

That question was answered the next morning, when upon her arrival at the

Hall Daisy spotted a bicycle propped against a side wall of the house. Oh no. Surely it couldn't be Chloe. Did she really hate Daisy that much?

As had happened the day before, Lex made a brief appearance to ask how she was getting on. Once she'd assured him all was well, he disappeared. She was aware of another, even stronger pang of disappointment — much to her disgust.

Then a couple of things happened to disturb Daisy's calm. The first was the arrival of Lex's wife, Annabel. 'I'm Lex's ex-wife. Who are you?' she demanded to know in a distinctly patronising tone.

'Well, and a good morning to you, too,' Daisy was tempted to respond. However, she managed to curb the impulse and instead said, with what she hoped was complete composure, 'I'm Daisy, Lex's new assistant.'

'Oh my God, not another one. You must be . . . now, let me count them up . . . oh yes, the eighth in six months. That's how long he's had an office at home. Tell me, do you think you'll be the first one to stay the course for longer than a couple of weeks?'

Daisy eyed the other woman's sardonic expression, trying to see what had attracted Lex to her. She was stick-thin, with eyes that were fully capable of cutting through steel, Daisy would have thought. Her mouth was so tightly compressed that her lips were barely visible.

'Well, I aim to try.'

But Annabel rudely cut her off. 'I need to speak to Lex about something. Where is he?'

'Um, I'm not sure. I think he went out.'

'Surely you, as his assistant, should know where he is. Otherwise, what use are you?'

Daisy was taken aback by the sheer bad manners of this woman. 'I'm not here to keep tabs on him. I just do his typing.'

'Really. Well, as you can't help me, I'll have to phone him and hope he's free to talk to me. It really is too bad.'

Daisy felt as if Lex's absence was in

some way her fault. So it was with a feeling of immense relief that she watched as Annabel flounced from the office without as much as a goodbye. She released a long, slow breath. No wonder Chloe was the way she was. She'd probably learnt her manners — or lack of them — from watching her mother in action.

The second event, mid-afternoon, was the arrival of two older people. Donna brought them into the office and Daisy sighed with exasperation. How on earth was she meant to get anything done? It wasn't her job to field visitors, surely, no matter who they might be?

'Daisy,' Donna began, 'sorry to interrupt, but these are Lex's parents, Marcus and Grace. They were passing, so . . . ' She shrugged her shoulders in a mute apology. 'Do you have any idea where Lex is?'

Daisy instantly got to her feet, wondering whether this day could possibly get any worse. This, then, was the elderly man that Grant had conned out of most of his money. She held out a hand. 'How do you do? I'm afraid I don't know where Lex is, and I'm not sure when he'll be back either.'

'Oh dear,' said Grace. She looked at her husband in noticeable exasperation. 'I told you we should ring first.' She turned back to Daisy and gave her a rueful smile. With her silver-grey hair and sparkling blue eyes, she was an attractive woman. In fact, Daisy thought she could see a lot of Lex in her.

'You did.' Marcus smiled gently. 'And as usual, my darling, you've been proved right.' He then looked at Daisy. 'We'll wait, Miss — '

'Lewis. Daisy Lewis.'

'Nice to meet you, Miss Lewis.'

'Oh, Daisy — please.'

'Daisy.' And he smiled again.

He really was charming, Daisy decided. Well, they both were. And, more importantly, there was no indication of recognition in their gazes. 'I'm sure Donna will make you a drink,' she told them. 'You could then maybe ring Lex.'

She raised a quizzical eyebrow at the housekeeper, who immediately said, 'Of course. Perhaps you'd both like to move into the drawing room? It's more comfortable.'

Once they'd gone, Daisy again reflected on what a charming couple they were — which resurrected her feelings of guilt over what Grant had done to them both. She shouldn't have agreed to take this job. If ever Lex discovered her true identity . . . She'd have to hand in her notice. Today. It felt deceitful and underhanded to continue to work for him, married as she'd been to Grant, the man responsible for his parents' financial loss. Yet, she needed a job.

However, as Lex hadn't returned by the time she left — considerably later than usual, as she'd wanted to finish one particular task before she went home — she was thwarted in her attempt to resign. It was as she was leaving the house that she spotted Chloe and Imogen walking towards it. They must have returned on the bus that was just pulling away from the end of the driveway. Daisy felt her heart give an almighty and sickening lurch. Now what?

12

It was Chloe who first spotted her. 'What are you doing here?' the girl furiously yelled.

Daisy's first thought was that Lex hadn't told his daughters that she was working for him. Her next was to wonder why not. He must have realised there was every chance that at some point they'd all meet up. Or maybe he'd hoped they wouldn't. Or could it be that he simply didn't care?

'I-I'm working for your father.'

'You're kidding! I knew he'd offered you the job,' Chloe burst out. 'I heard him on the phone to you. But I really, really thought you'd have the good sense to turn him down.'

As caution seemed her only option at that point, all Daisy said was, 'Why would I turn him down? I need a job.' She didn't know what else to say. What the girl's remarks did do, though, was renew her suspicion that Chloe might be her blackmailer; though she couldn't have known, when it all started, that her father would actually offer Daisy a job. Maybe she should demand to know if Chloe was the one responsible for everything that was happening to her. But supposing she wasn't? She'd then most likely want to know what Daisy was talking about. And that was something Daisy didn't want to be forced to reveal, not if she didn't have to.

'Need a job?' Chloe cried. 'You must be desperate then, knowing how I feel about you. I promise you, I can — and will — make your life totally unbearable.' Her expression was one of complete scorn now. 'And if you've got any other plans for my dad, like marriage, you can just forget them.'

'Chloe.' Imogen was tugging at her older sister's arm. 'Don't be rude. Dad wouldn't like it.'

'I'm sure he wouldn't, especially if he's already got something going with this-this slag.'

'Girls,' a voice called from the open doorway. The three of them swung round. It was Grace. Daisy hadn't realised the older couple were still there.

'What's going on? I could hear you shouting from the house, Chloe. Are you being rude to Miss Lewis?'

Chloe didn't respond, other than to sweep her gaze back to Daisy. But something flickered in her eyes and this time it wasn't scorn. It looked like apprehension, fear even; fear that Daisy would repeat all that she'd said to her grandmother. She wasn't much more than a child still, after all, despite the fact that her behaviour suggested someone a great deal older.

Even so, for a split second Daisy was tempted to do just that, to repeat the conversation to the older woman. But then she saw the way Chloe was looking at her, pleadingly almost, and she knew she couldn't do it. So all she said was, 'It's okay, Mrs Harper. We're just getting to know each other.' She turned back to Chloe and surprised a look of grudging respect, and maybe the merest hint of remorse. But whatever it was, the expression was swiftly gone again.

'Come on, Chloe,' Imogen muttered. 'You'll get us both into trouble.'

Daisy smiled down at the younger girl and said, 'Goodbye, Imogen,' before slanting a glance at Chloe and saying, 'You won't be seeing me again.' To her astonishment, Chloe looked horrified. 'I'll phone your father later and tell him. Don't worry.'

Chloe's look of horror deepened, and Daisy realised she thought she meant she'd tell Lex what his daughter had said. She didn't add anything more, however, just walked quickly to her car and climbed in. It wouldn't hurt the girl to worry a little. In fact, it might teach her to respect other people's feelings.

However, as Daisy drove away from the Hall, she felt her own apprehension increasing. What was Lex going to say when she told him she wouldn't be returning? Initially he'd be surprised, she was certain of that; surprised that a woman would actually refuse him something. But she imagined that his emotions would swiftly turn to anger, and possibly even disgust. She could already hear him: 'I didn't realise you were a quitter.'

Oh God. And she needed the job quite badly. But she couldn't go on working for him, not knowing how his eldest daughter felt about her. She deeply resented being labelled a slag. But more than that, much more, was her guilt about Marcus having lost most of his money to Grant.

* * *

It was eight o'clock that evening before she mustered up the courage to ring Lex.

'Hi,' was his warm greeting. 'How did your day go? I've had a look at all you've done, and I have to say, I'm impressed.'

'I won't be coming back,' she blurted.

'What?' There was a second's silence, then, 'Why not? There's still heaps to do.'

'Yes, I know, but I feel . . . '

'What?'

'Well, I don't think I'm up to the job.'

'Rubbish. As I've just said, you've done excellent work.' There was a moment's silence before he quietly asked, 'What's the real reason, Daisy?'

This was precisely what she'd dreaded. What the hell could she say? She couldn't tell him what Chloe had said. He'd really despise her then for allowing a teenage girl to drive her away. But all of a sudden, she realised she had the perfect excuse. 'My parents are coming tomorrow for an extended visit, and-and I really need to be here for them.' She swallowed, convinced he'd see straight through that. He'd already proved more than once how perceptive he could be. Let's face it, he'd just done it: he'd known she wasn't giving him the real reason for her resignation.

'Do you? Why? Are they not capable of looking after themselves for a few hours a day?'

'Well, yes, of course, but there's ALSO Ollie. He hasn't liked me not being around.'

Again there was a short silence. 'I

251

see.' He didn't sound angry with her, which was unexpected. But it didn't take her long to understand why that was. 'Okay, if that's the way you want it, so be it. At least it means I'll be able to see you socially. Or is that off the cards too for the moment?'

She cast her eyes heavenward. He always had an answer. The man was incorrigible. 'I'm afraid so. I'll be rather tied up.'

'Hmmm, sounds intriguing,' he then murmured. 'Who's going to be doing the tying? Not Ben Penter, I hope.' His tone noticeably hardened.

'Good Lord, no. You know what I mean.'

He relented. She could tell by his voice, which was laced with humour. 'Yes, I do. Okay. Well, I'll be seeing you then.'

Daisy almost blurted, 'Not if Chloe has anything to do with it.' However, she stayed silent and he could make what he wanted of that.

'I mean it, Daisy. I'm not giving up on you.'

A warmth began to spread its tentacles through her, only to be swiftly replaced by a sense of unutterable dejection. How could she possibly become romantically involved with him, with all she had to hide? Come to that, how could she become involved with any man?

* * *

The following afternoon Daisy's parents, Eve and Tom, arrived. The boot and back seat of their car was packed with luggage and boxes of provisions, including several bottles of wine. A happy distraction from yesterday's troubles.

'My goodness,' Daisy exclaimed, 'how long have you come for?'

Eve eyed her. 'Well, two or three weeks. Is that okay, darling? We really couldn't come empty-handed, knowing your financial situation at the moment.'

'Of course it's okay. How did you get here so early? I wasn't expecting you until much later.'

'We left well before it was light. We wanted to get here as soon as we could.' Her mother eyed her anxiously. 'We're not too early — ?'

'No, of course not. I've been looking forward to it.'

And she had been. The notion of company for the increasingly wintry nights was a welcome one, especially as last night had been particularly stormy. She'd lain in bed, nervously listening as the windows rattled noisily in their frames beneath the buffeting of the driving rain and the screaming gale-force wind. It had felt as if draughts were forcing their way in through every crack, whining eerily as they did so. In fact, it had been so bad that Daisy had expected the roof to be ripped off at any moment. Thankfully, she'd woken the next morning to nothing more threatening than a spirited breeze and a weak sun.

'Ollie,' she now called, 'come and meet the parents.' Ollie had been asleep upstairs somewhere, probably on her bed; his favourite spot. It was a wonder he hadn't heard the sounds of the car pulling up.

'We'll take ourselves off regularly so

that we're not under each other's feet,' her father said. 'We may even go off somewhere for two or three days, further down the coast. Mousehole's charming, we hear. You wouldn't mind, would you?'

'Of course not. It's your holiday.' But her spirits did sink at the thought of being left alone again, even for a mere three days. 'Let's get you unpacked, then after lunch we can all walk into town. There's plenty of time, and the shops will still be open. And you can stretch your legs. Then we'll get something more substantial to eat than a sandwich. There're some good pubs and restaurants. You can meet some of my friends, too.' She eyed her mother. 'Don't forget I'm known as Daisy now. Daisy Lewis.'

'Of course we won't. Really, Daisy, we're not stupid.'

★ ★ ★

'Pencarrow's just as I remember it,' Eve gleefully cried as they walked along Fore Street. As Daisy had promised, and as it was only half past four, most of the shops were still open. 'I was worried it might have been spoiled, as so many coastal towns have been.'

Tom said, 'I seem to remember there's a town quay, isn't there?'

'Yes — come on, let's go and have a look,' Daisy said. 'That's exactly the same too.'

With the quay duly inspected and pronounced slightly longer than it was twenty years ago — according to Tom, that was — Daisy took them back along the road to Freya's shop.

'Freya,' she called upon opening the door and finding the place empty, 'it's me, Daisy.'

The door behind the counter opened and Freya popped her head out. 'Oh, it's you. Sorry, I was doing the accounts while it's quiet.' Her gaze wandered to Eve and Tom.

'Meet my parents,' Daisy said. 'They're here for a couple of weeks — well, maybe a bit longer.'

Freya wasted no time in striding out

from behind the counter, holding out her hand as she did so. 'So nice to meet you. I was beginning to seriously wonder whether Daisy actually had any family. She hasn't said much at all about you.'

'Hasn't she?' Eve gave Daisy a faintly disapproving look. 'Well, I'm Eve, and this is Tom.'

'Great. Well, I hope you have a nice stay. The cottage is a bit out of the way,' she added, pulling a face, 'but if you like peace and quiet, you've come to the right place.'

'We've noticed that,' Eve said. 'It'll suit us perfectly. We'll get plenty of exercise, and that's no bad thing, not with all this gorgeous sea air. And if we want it, as you've said, plenty of peace and solitude. Now, where do you live, Freya? Near to Daisy?'

'Oh no, the opposite end of town.'

'Do you two girls get together much?'

'When we can,' Freya told her. 'I'm rather busy at the moment. By the way, Daisy, don't forget the rehearsal tomorrow.'

'I've joined the local am drama group,' she told her parents, before turning back to Freya and saying, 'I don't think I'll be able to make it tomorrow. But next week, definitely.'

Freya looked annoyed, and her tone reflected it. 'Too busy this week, are we?'

'Well, as you can see, my parents are here.'

'And, of course, she's got her job now,' Eve put in.

'Oh, what job's that then?' Freya asked, staring rather hard at Daisy.

Daisy bit her lip. Oh God. Now she was in for it. 'Um, I've been doing some work for Lex.'

Freya didn't say anything for a full minute. Then she remarked to Eve in a cloyingly chummy tone, 'Well, I must say, I'm full of admiration for your daughter. She isn't half a fast worker when she puts her mind to it.' She returned her attention to Daisy, either not seeing or disregarding Eve's surprised expression and slightly raised eyebrows. 'What have you been doing for him? Attending to his home comforts?' She was smiling, but her tone now was distinctly waspish, and Daisy, for one, couldn't mistake the innuendo. She just hoped her parents hadn't picked up on it.

'No, he wanted some computer work done.' She almost added, 'Not that it's any of your business,' but bit her tongue instead. Really, she was growing a little weary of Freya's increasingly frequent displays of jealousy. However, as she had no wish to provoke a row in front of her parents, she said nothing. It wasn't any of her doing that two of the evidently most eligible men in the town were showing their preference for her.

'Really? Computer work?'

'Yes,' Eve said. 'Daisy's very good at that sort of thing. I'm hopeless. Don't even possess one, do we, Tom?' She gave a chuckle. 'Daisy's his PA.'

'Really? His PA? How interesting. That's his personal assistant, isn't it?' Freya's eyes were practically shooting darts of venom at Daisy by this time.

'Tell me, Daisy, how personal has it been so far?'

Eve gave a tinkly laugh as finally she picked up on Freya's sarcasm. 'It's not personal in the sense you mean, Freya.'

'No? Is that right, Daisy?'

'Yes, and it was only for a couple of days, in any case. I wouldn't really describe myself as a PA.' She sensed her mother's surprised glance at her. No wonder, as she'd told her that it would be a permanent position — which, of course, was what she herself had expected it to be. Her mistake, she now conceded, had been not getting round to telling Eve that it hadn't worked out. She should have anticipated her mother would blurt out the news at the first opportunity. It was from her, after all, that Daisy had inherited her own wayward tongue.

Freya didn't bother to respond to this. Instead, she looked at Eve once more. 'What are you planning to do with yourselves while you're here?'

Eve, looking heartily relieved at the

ordinariness of the question, said, 'Well, we thought we might pay a visit to Mousehole next week and stay a couple of nights. We've never been. Maybe Wednesday and Thursday, then return to Daisy on Friday. That'll leave her free to go to your rehearsal.'

'Good, good. Well, I don't wish to be inhospitable, but I do have loads to do.' Freya pointedly indicated the office door behind her.

'Of course,' Eve politely said, taking the massive hint on the chin. 'I hope we'll meet again. We could all have a drink together at the cottage one evening, maybe.' She smiled hopefully, clearly having decided to forget the momentary hostility between the two younger women, or completely ignore it. Eve was an expert at disregarding anything even remotely unpleasant. She'd even managed to ignore Grant's disappearance for a while, telling Daisy, 'He'll soon be back, tail between his legs,' which Daisy had found incomprehensible. Her mother surely couldn't be seriously expecting him to return and for Daisy to take him back? And what about his crime? The police certainly wouldn't ignore that. No, she'd accepted that she wouldn't be seeing Grant again. Eventually, of course, Eve had also accepted what had happened and, as a consequence, did all she could to comfort and help her daughter.

'We've brought plenty of supplies with us, haven't we, Dar — '

Daisy glared at her mother, who had almost said 'Darcey'.

Eve hastily corrected herself. 'Um — darling.'

Freya didn't seem to have noticed the slip and said, 'Well maybe, if Daisy can find the time to entertain. All these men so eager to spend time with her.'

Eve looked bewildered again, and her daughter sighed. If Freya only knew there was no possibility of Daisy involving herself with any man. Maybe she should tell Freya that, but then she'd have to also tell her that she was already married. And knowing how up on local gossip Freya was, there was every chance that she'd mention it to someone, and then that someone would pass it on, and hey presto — the whole damned town would know. Not that that really mattered, Daisy supposed; there was nothing incriminating about her being married. But her private life was exactly that, private, and that was the way she wanted to keep it.

Another question raised its head then. She'd told Lex she was married. Supposing he mentioned it? Oh well, it was too late now. She'd just have to deal with it if and when it happened. Till then, she wouldn't worry.

'Come on, we'll leave Freya to her accounting and I'll introduce you to Leah Bennett, another good friend,' she said to her parents. She glanced back at Freya, but the other woman was already disappearing into her office at the rear of the shop.

Leah, when Daisy introduced her parents, was altogether different from Freya. She looked genuinely delighted to meet them. A smile wreathed her face as she enthusiastically shook their hands. 'How lovely to meet you. You must be thrilled to have them here, Daisy. That cottage is a bit isolated for a woman on her own.'

Daisy wished people wouldn't keep harping on about that. All it did was intensify her nervousness, even now that she had Ollie. She glanced down at her pet. He was so well-behaved, patiently sitting and waiting for them to move on.

'How long are you staying?'

'Two or three weeks.' It was Eve once more who spoke. Tom seemed more intent on looking around him than carrying on any sort of conversation. He was contentedly browsing amongst the paintings. 'If Daisy can put up with us for that long.' She smiled warmly at her daughter. 'I told Freya we're planning a couple of jaunts away from Pencarrow. Wednesday and Thursday nights. It'll give Daisy a little break from us.'

'Mum, you know I don't need a break from you,' Daisy gently protested. 'I'm going to love having you stay.'

'Yes, it's a pity, really. If you'd still been working for Lex Harper, you wouldn't have noticed we'd gone.'

Daisy sighed. Pretty soon the entire town would know who she'd been working for.

'You've been working for Lex?' Leah picked up instantly on that piece of news. In fact, her ears all but twitched. Her eyes definitely gleamed.

'Yes, only for a couple of days,' Daisy told her, somehow managing to hide her resigned amusement at her friend's reaction to the news. 'I did a bit of computer work for him, that's all. It's nothing to get excited about.'

'Nothing to get excited about?' Leah cried. 'If it had been me in that position, I'd have taken out an ad in the local paper. Anything to broadcast my immense luck. Wow, working for that gorgeous man! I'd have done it for free. In fact, if I'm honest, I would have paid him for the privilege.'

Eve, too, was struggling to hide her smiles by this time. She glanced curiously at her daughter and archly asked, 'Do I take it he's something special then?'

'Special?' Leah again cried. 'There isn't a woman in town who wouldn't give their eye teeth to be working for Lex, and this woman here — ' She pointed to Daisy. ' — says it's nothing to get excited about.'

Eve really did laugh then. 'You didn't tell me all this, Daisy.'

'No, Mum, because there was nothing to tell. It was a job, and now it's over. End of story,' she curtly concluded.

Leah eyed her knowingly. 'Did you happen to meet Chloe, by any chance, while you were there?'

'I did, yes.' And that was all she was going to say on that subject.

Eve was looking from one to the other of them, frankly puzzled.

'Who's Chloe? Lex's wife?'

'No, his daughter,' Leah told her. 'She's a leeeetle bit possessive of her father. In fact, you could reasonably liken her to a particularly fierce Rottweiler when any

266

woman comes closer than six inches to Lex. He's divorced from her mother, you see.'

Daisy decided it was time she interrupted this particular topic of conversation. 'We're going to have to leave you, Leah. I promised Mum and Dad I'd take them to the Ship for a meal. What's the food like?'

'Good; very good. Gets busy later on, so you're right, it's best to go early. Well, it's been a delight to meet you both.' She once again grabbed hold of their hands.

'I'm sure we'll see you around,' Eve told her. 'Pencarrow's not a large town. I must take a look at the paintings, too, before we leave again.'

They finally managed to take their leave and headed for the Ship. 'What lovely friends you have, darling,' Eve told Daisy. 'We should have a little party while your dad and I are here. What do you think?'

'Mum, I don't know enough people yet to have a party.'

'Well, what about your drama group? You know them. And then there's Lex Harper. I'd love to meet him and see what all the fuss is about.' She slanted a sly look towards her daughter at that point.

Daisy grimaced to herself. Her mother had always been able to see straight through her. She'd obviously detected her attraction to Lex and now was set upon a spot of matchmaking. Along with Leah, she suspected. 'No, Mum. I'm not ready for a party.' She needed first of all to find out who was trying to blackmail her. Until she knew that, she was letting no one inside the walls of Blue Haven.

13

The following days passed peacefully and uneventfully, to Daisy's relief. There were no anonymous phone calls, no more threatening letters, no stones through windows, no one standing in the dark staring at the cottage. She found herself wondering once again if her persecutor knew she had guests and so was leaving her alone, which did seem to disturbingly point to the culprit being one of her friends.

Before she knew it, a week had gone by, and she was seeing her parents off on their visit to Mousehole. They'd decided to add a visit to Marazion and St Michael's Mount while they were at it. 'Have a good time,' she called.

'We will,' Eve called back, waving one hand through the open window. 'See you Friday sometime — probably late afternoon.'

Daisy went back inside the cottage, resigning herself to the unnerving prospect of spending the next three days and two nights alone. Still, she consoled herself, she had the rehearsal to go to tomorrow evening, so that would take her mind off things. Today, she decided, she'd take herself off to the nearby town of St Austell and a spot of shopping. She needed some more clothes, although not the smarter workday suits she'd planned to buy. Instead, she purchased more jeans and some thick sweaters. The November days were growing increasingly cold, and more often than not damp. So with that in mind, she also bought a thermally lined waterproof jacket, something she'd definitely need for her walks with Ollie. She eventually ended up in a small café, where she ordered and consumed a large plateful of battered cod and chips. No need now to prepare herself her usual solitary meal.

It was already dark by the time she returned home. The first thing she noticed was the broken kitchen window — again — and then the sound of Ollie barking. Oh God, was someone inside the cottage?

She leapt from the car and ran to the front door, her main concern for her pet. The door was undamaged and still locked, so if anyone was in there they'd have to have climbed through the window. Taking into account the jagged splinters of glass that still remained attached to the wooden frame, however, that would have been a perilous exercise. Of course, they could have attempted it via the rear windows.

Bearing that thought in mind, Daisy quietly unlocked the door and crept into the hallway. Ollie was right there, crouched on the floor, ears flat against his head. He leapt to his feet instantly, whining and wagging his tail.

'Okay, I'm back. What happened, eh?'

Gingerly, and with Ollie at her heels, she first peered into the kitchen. Finding no signs of an intruder there, she went into the sitting room and switched on the exterior arc lights that were fixed to the back wall of the cottage. Nothing appeared to be damaged or missing from outside. She glanced around the room. Nothing appeared to be missing from in here either. Once again, whoever it had been had made no attempt to get inside, either through the kitchen window or by way of the garden by climbing over the wall that divided the cottage from the beach.

With Ollie at her heels she returned to the kitchen. Yet again, it looked as if the attacker had simply wanted to smash the glass, like last time. There were glass splinters all over the table top, again just like last time, but no large stone. Either they'd used something else, or they'd taken it away with them.

She then proceeded to search the up-stairs rooms, just in case; but as she'd expected she found nothing out of the ordinary there either, and she returned to the hallway. Maybe there was a note, but there was nothing on the doormat.

It all added to her growing belief that this was all about terrorising her, punishing her, rather than extorting money; money the blackmailer must know by this time she hadn't got. This was someone intent on making her life a misery, or possibly driving her away. Again, she wondered about Chloe. It would suit her to force Daisy to leave the town and thus her father.

Daisy didn't bother calling the police. Instead she cleared up the broken glass and covered the window with the same sheet of cardboard she'd used last time. She'd call the glazier first thing in the morning.

Eventually she poured herself a much-needed gin and tonic; and feeling in need of the comfort that a fire would bring, she lit the log-burner in the sitting room. She then sat as close to it as she could, and slowly sipped her drink while contemplating what she should do. The person responsible for all that was happening clearly wasn't going to stop.

She sighed. 'Oh Ollie, what am I

going to do?' He cocked his head to one side and whined. 'I know, I feel the same way.' Maybe she should ring someone to come and keep her company. But who? Freya? No, she was in such an odd mood lately. Leah? She was a possibility.

But the decision was taken out of her hands when her mobile rang. She picked it up and saw that it was Lex calling. She hesitated, her finger hovering over the keypad. What could he want? Had he decided recriminations were in order, after all? She had let him down rather badly on the job front. But what could he say to her, really? Huh, what couldn't he?

She answered with a slightly nervous, 'Hello?'

'Hi. I wondered if you'd like to meet for a drink?'

Daisy was taken aback. That had been the last question she'd expected. 'Um, I-I can't.'

'Why not? Ollie will be okay for a while.'

'No, that's not the reason.' Her voice

wobbled as tears sprang into her eyes. Damn, damn, the last thing she wanted was for Lex Harper to hear her crying.

'Daisy? What's wrong? And don't say nothing, because I know that wouldn't be true.' His voice was gravelly and deep.

Good grief, he'd done it again, Daisy decided. He'd sussed out her thoughts, her very emotions. What was it with this man? Did nothing get past him? Had he got some sort of sixth sense?

'M-my kitchen window's been broken and I've only managed a temporary repair.' Her voice broke now, as her breath caught in her throat.

'Again?' His tone was a sharp one. 'What happened this time?'

'The same as last time. Probably a stone put through it, though I can't find one.'

'Are your parents not there?'

'No, they've gone off for a couple of days.'

'I'm coming round.'

'There's no need.'

But he'd ended the call. Daisy stared

at the phone and muttered, 'Okay, so you're coming round, then.' Almost at once, another problem presented itself. He would be bound to ask why someone would smash her window twice. Should she tell him the truth? She sighed. How could she, when his own father had lost so much money?

Within minutes, it felt, he was ringing her doorbell. How on earth had he got there so fast? She was beginning to seriously wonder about him. He certainly had some extraordinary powers. Not least, the ability to read her mind at will.

With a deep sense of misgiving, she opened the door to him, expecting to see him on the doorstep. There was no one there. Her heart gave an almighty lurch. Oh God, was it her blackmailer? Not content with simply breaking her window twice, was he now about to physically attack her?

Cautiously, she peered out and gave a huge gasp of relief. Lex was standing in front of the broken window, closely inspecting it. He spotted her at once. 'When did this happen?'

'Um, I'm not sure. I wasn't here; I was in St Austell. I returned to find it like this, and Ollie going mad.'

'Hmmm.' His glance was a keen one. 'Kids, do you think?'

'Oh, yes, well — goodness, I hadn't thought of that,' she heard herself gushing, so great was her relief. She hadn't had to tell any sort of lie; he'd come up with a perfectly acceptable reason for the damage himself. It was pure fiction, of course, but she couldn't help that. She couldn't bring herself to tell him the truth, she simply couldn't.

But he was staring at her even more keenly now, his narrowed gaze riveted to her face. It was as if he was searching for the truth. Had she overdone her enthusiasm for his theory? He certainly looked suspicious.

'Please, come in,' she said.

'I'm not disturbing you, am I?'

'Oh no. Ollie and I were just having a quiet night in.'

'Where have your parents gone?'

'Mousehole and then Marazion. Strangely, although we visited Cornwall several times years ago, we never went.' She tried a smile then — a shaky one, it was true, but at least she did manage it.

It didn't fool Lex for a second. 'So you were alone when you found the window?'

'Yes.' She ushered him into the sitting room and then turned back to face him. His stare was a quizzical one.

'I could stay the night if you're nervous.'

'Oh no,' she hastened to assure him. 'I'll be fine.' And in any case, where would he sleep? Her parents were occupying the only guest room and all their belongings were spread round it. Her mother wasn't the tidiest of people. Something else she'd inherited from her.

'You don't look it. You're very pale.' Lex reached out a hand to touch her cheek. She jumped as if he was holding a red-hot poker to her. 'My, my,' he softly said, 'you're nervy.'

'I wasn't expecting it, that's all. Please

— sit down.' She indicated the armchair.

'I'd rather sit there,' he said, pointing at the settee, 'by the side of you.'

He'd noticed the newspaper placed on one of the cushions, ready for her to open up and read. Swiftly, she picked it up and placed it on the coffee table. 'I'll sit on the chair,' she said. His proximity was doing all sorts of crazy things to her pulse rate, as well as her breathing. As was the scent of his aftershave. It filled her head, intoxicating, exhilarating, inspiring a desire she felt powerless to control. In fact, now she considered it, every single nerve ending that she possessed — and it felt like millions — was leaping with her need to have his arms about her.

'Am I making you nervous?' he asked.

Nervous? He was frightening the flippin' life out of her. Still, she managed to laugh lightly and then ask, 'Why would you?'

'You tell me,' he smoothly said. His gaze fastened itself onto her eyes before moving down to her mouth. It was as if he was touching her, caressing her. Her lips parted involuntarily as her breath snagged in her throat.

'Please,' she tried again, 'sit down.' This time she pointed at the settee.

He did as she asked, finally. Desperately trying to appear unconcerned at his presence here in her home, she turned and walked swiftly to the armchair.

'Daisy,' he murmured, 'come here.'

Her breathing quickened, her breasts rising and falling, as she turned to face him. He was holding out a hand to her. What should she do? Should she sit next to him, as he so obviously wanted? But what if he tried to kiss her? She wouldn't be able to resist him; she simply didn't possess the strength. And it was then that the truth finally dawned on her: she was falling in love with him. Falling in love? She *had* fallen in love. Deeply. Irrevocably. How could she have been so stupid?

'Come,' he again said, and this time it was an unmistakable command. His eyes gleamed from beneath lowered lids as he softly said, 'I won't eat you. At least, not yet.' His mouth curved into an outrageously sensuous smile.

Completely mesmerised by the sheer force of the desire she was experiencing, Daisy moved helplessly towards him. Quivering with anticipation, she lowered herself onto the settee to perch primly on the edge of the seat, too frightened to look at him for fear he'd detect the desire that was surging through her. Of course, it didn't fool him for a second. Why had she thought it would? He slid his arm around her waist and pulled her back, tucking her into his side. Her head nestled naturally into the hollow between his neck and his shoulder.

She looked up to find him staring down at her. 'There,' he huskily murmured, 'nothing to be afraid of.'

Huh, well, he would say that, wouldn't he? But if that was true, why did he have that hungry look? She blinked up at him. Who did he think he was kidding with his protestation of guilelessness? Certainly not her. The truth was, she was beginning to feel like the archetypical defenceless lamb about to be gobbled up by a big bad wolf: namely, Lex Harper.

But then he set about disproving her theory when he used his free hand to gently cup her chin and tilt her face up to his, whereupon he lowered his head and touched her mouth in the softest of kisses. She quite distinctly heard his swiftly indrawn breath the instant before he deepened the kiss, and without knowing quite how it happened she was being held tightly against him, her breasts flattened against his chest. Her lips parted beneath his as he murmured, 'Oh Daisy,' even as he continued to kiss her. His one arm tightened its grip until it felt as if their bodies had become one.

Daisy couldn't help herself; her hands crept upwards until her fingers were entwined at the back of his neck, their tips nestled in amongst the thickness of his hair. He groaned, his tongue thrusting in to open her lips even further. Now it was Daisy who groaned as her entire body responded to his passion.

Her insides burned with desire and a quite urgent need, and she realised she wanted this man as she'd never wanted a man before.

He pushed her backwards until she was all but lying beneath him on the settee. His one hand enclosed her breast to gently squeeze and fondle. She gave a low moan as his hand moved again and his fingers began to explore beneath the sweater she was wearing. It wasn't until they found their way onto naked flesh and slid across to the sensitised peak that the full realisation of what she was allowing struck her. At the same moment Ollie gave a low growl, and that was all it took to restore her to her senses. She pushed Lex off her and struggled to sit up, at the same time tugging her sweater back down over herself. Her skin burned with shame at what had just happened.

Lex had instantly released her. He stared at her from heavy-lidded eyes, his breathing coming fast and shallow. 'What's wrong?'

'You know what's wrong,' she burst out. 'Ssh, Ollie.' The dog was on his feet now, growling menacingly at Lex. 'It's okay. Sit.' Ollie ignored her. 'Ollie. Sit.' He did so, but kept his eyes fixed on Lex.

'No, I don't actually,' Lex said. His jawline had tightened as his gaze seared into her.

'I'm married,' she cried, 'which you know very well. I shouldn't be doing this.'

Lex's frowning gaze lightened then. 'Is that all?'

'Is that all? Isn't that enough?'

'Well, as I believe I said once before, you're separated. You don't know where he is to get a divorce.' He shrugged, dragging her gaze to the width of his shoulders, and thereby resurrecting her trembling desire. 'I would say that gives you a perfect right to have another relationship. He can't expect you to live like a nun.'

'You don't understand.' How could she start a relationship with him, with anyone, while she had such a hugely damaging secret? He didn't even know her real name.

'Well then, make me understand. Talk to me. I know you're as attracted to me as I am to you. We could be good together.'

'Could we? And what would Chloe have to say about that?'

'Chloe will have to live with it. What I do with my life is my concern.' His tone had hardened, as had his eyes as he continued to watch her. 'But that's not it, is it? There's something else going on here. Something that's stopping you. Look, I'll be honest — I'm falling in love with you, and I think . . . no, strike that; I *know* that it's the same for you. You couldn't have kissed me like you did if you didn't feel something for me, Daisy.' He gripped her gently by the shoulders. 'We could have such a good life together. A proper life. I'll find your husband if that's what it takes. Shouldn't be too difficult for the right people.'

'What?' she cried. 'What do you mean, the right people?'

'A private detective. I know one, a good one. I've used him before.'

'You have?' She stared at him, aghast at the implications of that final remark.

'Yes, to check out people's credentials before employing them or doing business with them. Believe me, Daisy, I'll find him. I want you, really want you.' His gaze burned into her. 'Daisy?'

'My name's not Daisy,' she blurted, only to instantly cover her mouth with her hand. What the hell had she done?

It was his turn to stare now. 'What is it, then?'

'Darcey. Darcey Carter. My husband is-is . . . ' She swallowed. Oh God. Would his love be extinguished once he knew the truth? Would he despise her? ' . . . Grant Carter.'

She watched as realisation slowly dawned. 'Grant Carter?' Anger gradually replaced the lingering traces of passion. 'The man who swindled hundreds of people out of their savings — my father, for one?'

Daisy nodded. She felt the blood draining from her face. She shrank back into the corner of the settee, as far from Lex as she could get, crossing her arms defensively across her breasts.

He continued to watch her, silent now, his skin as pale as hers must be. 'Did you know what he was doing? Did you help him, as the papers said?'

She shook her head. 'No, I had no idea. He never once spoke to me about his business. I-I didn't know until he ran out on me and left me practically destitute, with a mountain of debt.'

Lex raised an eyebrow at her. He didn't believe her. Daisy felt her heart thud sickeningly within her breast. He believed she was as crooked as Grant had been — either that, or he thought her incredibly stupid to be so duped.

'Did you never question his sudden accumulation of wealth? He had every-thing, or so the papers said — expensive cars, a yacht, a large house . . . '

'I know. He told me they were the rewards for investing well and working hard. I believed him.' A single tear forced itself from her eye and tracked its way down her cheek. She dashed it away. 'I've lost everything as well. The house, everything. I sold as much as I could, but Grant hadn't paid for most of it. It was all taken back. I was left with nothing. A few thousand pounds, that's all, and that's fast disappearing.' The tears were coming more rapidly now, streaming down her face to drip off her chin. She gave a small sob as she fought to stem them. She didn't succeed. Again, she tried to dash them away.

'My God,' Lex breathed. 'That's why you've come here to this out-of-the-way town, where no one would know you.'

She nodded. She was crying too hard to speak.

He leant forward and pulled her in to him once more. He wrapped his arms around her and rocked her back and forth, holding her close, safe, as he murmured, 'Ssh. Ssh.' Ollie sat quietly watching, as if he'd sensed his mistress's grief. 'Oh, Daisy — Darcey,' Lex swiftly corrected himself.

'Daisy's fine,' she gasped. 'I'm used to it and I quite like it. Well, actually, I prefer it.'

'Daisy.' Again, he cupped her chin in his hand and tilted her head back until she was forced to look directly at him. 'I promise we'll find him. Then you can divorce him and marry me.'

She pulled back, her expression one of utter disbelief. 'What?'

'I love you, I told you, and I believe you when you say you knew nothing about Grant's scheme.'

'B-but — '

'We won't tell anyone who you are.'

'Someone knows.'

Lex looked astonished. 'They do? Who?'

'I don't know.' And she related all that had been happening to her.

'So the twice-broken window is down to this unknown person?'

'I think so. There was no letter this time, though.'

'Right.' He looked frighteningly grim now. 'It's imperative that we discover who it is, and then we deal with them.'

14

With that decided, Lex went on to say, 'I'll stay the night here.'

'What about your girls?'

'They're at their mother's until the weekend, so that's fine. I'll sleep on the settee. Okay?' He raised an expectant eyebrow at her, but Daisy didn't respond; *couldn't* respond, if the truth was known. Her brain was whirling madly as she tried to take everything in. Lex loved her; he wanted to marry her.

'I'll stay until your parents return,' he then declared. 'As for now, forget it all. I need to make love to you.' He stopped talking then. 'There's something else, though. Something I need to know.'

'What?' She swallowed nervously. Had he had second thoughts already about becoming entangled in her mess? She wouldn't blame him if he had.

'You haven't told me how you feel

about me.' He raised that same eyebrow at her.

'I feel the same as you.'

'You do? Could you please say it then? I-I really need to hear the words.'

'I love you. I tried to stop, but I couldn't.'

He gave a soft sigh. 'Thank God for that. So, with that cleared up, come here.' He yanked her in to him, holding her close as he began to kiss her again, extremely thoroughly and very passionately. So much so, she was left in no doubt that he'd meant what he said. He loved her, totally and absolutely.

There was also something else she had no doubt about: her blackmailer wasn't Lex. The relief that accompanied that realisation was huge. Her world, which had been so rocked by doubts and suspicions, righted itself as, for the first time in months, she felt safe, secure, and finally at peace.

★　★　★

Daisy awoke the next morning to the sound of raindrops hurling themselves against the bedroom window and wind howling around the house. Winter had clearly and noisily arrived for real. But she didn't care; she was far too happy to let a bit of stormy weather get her down. She smiled and regarded the man lying next to her, before sighing rapturously and snuggling into his side. She suspected that he'd had no intention of spending the night on the settee. He'd planned this, without a doubt. She grinned even more broadly, especially when his arm snaked around her and he murmured, 'Good morning, my love. How are you?' His eyes opened then and Daisy gloried in the love she saw gleaming there. She leant into him and kissed him.

'Oh, Daisy, Daisy, I could stay here all day with you, but I have to go. I've got several appointments I really can't miss. But apart from that, I have to get that private detective started. He needs to get cracking. We've no time to waste.

I want us to be together, properly.'

He eventually left, promising to call her and let her know he'd set the hunt for Grant in motion. 'I'll see you this evening,' he said.

'Oh, I've just remembered I've got the am' dram' rehearsal,' she said. 'I can't let them down. If I do, my name will be mud, at least as far as Freya's concerned. I had to miss it last week; my parents had just arrived.'

'Okay. What time does it finish? I'll come round then.'

With that agreed, they parted, and Daisy dressed to go walking with Ollie, who seemed to have accepted Lex's presence in the cottage. Once their walk was over, Daisy proceeded to busy herself tidying the cottage, a task she'd neglected for too long.

She eventually left for the town hall in her car at six fifteen. Lex had forbidden her to walk. 'If someone's stalking you, then it's not safe. If I could be sure I'd be back in time, I'd take you.' He had a late appointment, however, and wouldn't be home till nine o'clock-ish, maybe half past. She'd be home by then. Rehearsals only lasted a couple of hours — for her, at least, as her part was so small. The others would probably stay longer.

'Don't worry,' she assured him, 'I'll drive.' She'd made no mention of her suspicions about Chloe and her possible part in all that had been happening. That was Daisy's chief concern — that the culprit would turn out to be Lex's daughter.

As luck had it, she managed to find a parking place on the town quay, from where it was a hop and a jump to the hall. She walked in to a chorus of 'Nice to see you — to see you, nice.' She grinned around at them all. 'I'm sorry I had to miss last week's rehearsal. I've got visitors, in case anyone doesn't know.' Which, given the way gossip circulated around this town, seemed highly unlikely.

She was hugely relieved that no one seemed upset about her absence the previous week. She glanced around now, searching for Freya, and finally spotted her sitting in a corner, apparently immersed in the script to the exclusion of everything else.

'Hi,' Daisy called over. 'Are you okay?'

Freya simply grunted in response. Daisy pulled a face. 'Obviously not forgiven then for missing last week?' she muttered. Honestly, what was Freya's problem? It wasn't as if Daisy had a big part. She knew her lines and she knew how to say them.

'Hey, Freya. I saw you yesterday at about half past five,' a man's voice called. It was Daisy's nearest neighbour, Johnnie. 'It looked as if you were heading for Daisy's cottage. Going for tea, were you? We don't often see you our side of town. You should have called on us as well. Sandra would have liked to see you. We don't get many visitors.'

Yet again, Freya declined to answer. In fact, she looked even more intently at the pages of script. Daisy stared at her. Freya had been heading for the cottage? She wondered if she'd seen anyone hanging around, and strode over to her.

'Freya, can I ask you something? Someone broke my kitchen window yesterday afternoon while I was out, and not for the first time. Did you see anyone? Kids, anyone at all? It was probably done about the time you were there.'

For a second she thought Freya was going to ignore her, but then she asked, still looking at her script rather than Daisy, 'Why would someone do that? Have you made an enemy here, Daisy? Someone you've upset, maybe?'

'I'm not aware of having upset anyone.' She paused. 'Other than you, that is. You've been a bit cool with me. Not to say downright hostile at times.' She was beginning to feel uneasy. Freya was behaving in a very odd fashion, even more so than usual.

Freya looked up at her then, her face twisted as she hissed, 'Why don't you repay all the money you and your miserable thieving husband stole? And don't try and tell me you don't know where he is, living it up with my gran's and everybody else's cash, because I won't believe you. No one will believe you.'

'What? I don't know where — Oh my God,' Daisy gasped. 'It's been you. All along. All of it. You knew who I was.' She felt as if someone had punched her in the stomach. She couldn't breathe, and pressed a hand to her chest as she began to gasp for air.

'That's right,' Freya softly said. 'The very first time you came into my shop, I recognised you right away. I'd kept cuttings from the papers; photos. I hoped one day I'd see you somewhere, you and your thieving bastard of a husband. I couldn't believe it when you actually walked into my shop, and so soon after it all. It seemed like Fate had intervened, and I knew I had to do something — make you suffer like my gran did, knowing she had no money left after you stole it from her. I lost her because of you, you bitch. And now you're helping yourself to Lex. I saw you kissing him the other evening. You were all over him; it was nauseating.'

'Everything okay over there?' Leah called.

'Yes, fine,' Daisy managed to answer, albeit shakily. 'We're just having a chat.' She looked back at Freya. 'I did nothing, Freya. I knew nothing about what Grant was doing.'

'Yeah, right. Puh-leese. How could you not know?'

'Easily. I barely saw him for that last year or so.'

'And you didn't wonder what he was up to? Where all the money was coming from to pay for all the luxuries? The big house, the yacht, the car? Are you really that stupid?'

'I don't think so. I believed him when he said he'd invested wisely. Why wouldn't I? I-I even thought he was having an affair — which he was.' She eyed Freya then. 'How did you know

I'd be out yesterday?'

'I didn't. I knocked on your door. When you didn't answer . . . ' She shrugged.

'What would you have done if I'd been there?'

'Invited myself in. Said I was out having a walk and was passing — which I was, actually — and thought I'd call in. Again true. When I realised you were out, it seemed too good an opportunity to pass up. There was nobody around.'

'You terrified me. How could you?' Daisy said.

'Easily. You're pathetic. I don't believe you didn't know what he was doing. No one could be that blind, that gullible. You should have done something, you silly cow. Stopped him.' She brought her hand up and slapped Daisy hard across the face, first on one side, then the other. Daisy put a defensive hand up, trying to protect herself from the stinging blows.

'Hey, hey, stop that! What the hell's going on here?' It was an ashen-faced

Leah. 'What are you doing Freya, slapping poor Daisy?'

'Poor Daisy?' Freya cried, giving a screech of laughter. 'You are joking. Haven't you realised who poor Daisy really is?' He tone was one of scathing contempt. 'Haven't any of you recognised her? Her face was all over the papers, for God's sake. Don't you read, any of you?'

'What do you mean, who Daisy really is?' Leah was beginning to look a little uncertain now. Wildly, she glanced back and forth between Daisy and Freya. 'What are you on about, Freya?'

'Freya, please don't,' Daisy softly pleaded. 'Don't do this. I've told you the truth. I didn't know.'

'Do you want another slap? Will that make you admit your crime?' However, she limited herself to pushing Daisy this time. Nonetheless, it was hard enough so that Daisy staggered backwards and only just stopped herself from falling. 'Tell us the truth, you cow. You did know.'

'Will someone please tell me what's

going on?' It was Leah again, but by this time everyone was looking across at them.

'Gladly. Hey, everyone,' Freya shouted, 'Daisy's Grant Carter's wife. Yeah, that's right. The man who swindled a lot of us out of all of our money. My gran out of her money; every penny of it. The man who caused her death. She's Darcey Carter. That's her real name. She's deceived us all — except me, that is. I recognised her the second I saw her, despite her having dyed her hair and changed her name.'

Daisy heard Leah's gasp. 'Daisy, is that right?'

Daisy nodded. Everyone was murmuring and moving towards them.

'Did you know what he was doing?' Leah then asked.

'No, of course I didn't.'

'You're a liar,' Freya burst out. 'Put up your hands, everyone who lost money to the wonderful Carters.'

No one did.

Daisy gave a low moan before fearfully glancing around. Everyone was clustered about her now. She saw Ben, his expression one of deep shock, despite his original suspicion that he knew her. Johnny Larson, too, looked astonished. In fact, everyone looked genuinely shocked and appalled. The murmurings started up again. Daisy wrapped her arms tightly about herself as she struggled to control the deep-seated shudders that were threatening to tear her apart. What if they turned on her and attacked her, all of them? She wouldn't stand a chance.

'I'm sorry,' she cried, 'but I truly didn't know what Grant was doing. I wasn't involved. I lost everything, too. My home, almost everything I owned — I had to change my name, my appearance. I was being hounded by the press, as well as local people.'

'People you'd defrauded, presumably?' Freya spat.

Leah was the first to break rank, and put her arm around Daisy. 'You poor, poor thing.' Other murmurings of sympathy followed.

'If I could repay the money I would,' Daisy said in a shaky voice.

'So why don't you?' Freya spat. 'Words are easy; words cost nothing. Tell the police where your thieving husband is. They can get our money back then.'

'Freya, isn't it obvious that Daisy doesn't have the money to pay anyone back?' Leah angrily demanded. 'Be reasonable. Does she look like a wealthy woman to you? And I'm sure if she knew where her husband was, she'd have told the police weeks ago.'

'Shall I call the police?' someone now piped up.

'Please,' Daisy pleaded, 'please don't.'

'Why not?' Freya sneered at her. 'Afraid they'll arrest you?'

'No. I was cleared of any blame. Totally cleared.'

It was Ben who spoke then. 'You can't really believe Daisy was part of the scam, Freya. I certainly don't. In my opinion, she doesn't have a dishonest bone in her body.'

Daisy looked at Freya, who stared

defiantly back. It was as if she was challenging Daisy to bring in the police. Daisy didn't respond, other than to say, 'Let's get on with the rehearsal, shall we? That's why we're here, after all.'

Leah enthusiastically endorsed that. 'Yes, that's a very good idea. It'll give everyone time to cool down. But I want it known for the record that I totally believe Daisy when she says she knew nothing of what her husband was doing.'

The only response to that declaration was a loud and scornful snort from Freya, though there were one or two hear-hears from the other group members that cheered Daisy considerably. Clearly not everyone was condemning her and labelling her a fraudster.

It wasn't until they'd all taken up their positions for the opening scene that Daisy whispered, 'Freya, I won't report the things you've been doing to me if it all stops now. I haven't got any money; Grant took the lot and ran away. If I had, I'd gladly pay some back, though how I'd set about doing that I don't know. I've no idea who lost money. And as for Lex and me, well, I'm sorry, truly. But we love each other.'

Freya shrugged her shoulders; it was as if her anger had evaporated as quickly as it had arisen. Maybe she realised she'd gone way over the top, and that the rest of the group didn't share her venomous feelings towards Daisy. 'Does Lex know the truth about you?' she murmured.

'Yes, I've told him everything.' Daisy decided not to mention the matter of the private detective. That was no one else's business.

Freya didn't speak for a moment. Then all she said was, 'Well, I hope they catch him. I need to see him in jail for what he's done.'

'You and me both. So — friends?' Daisy held out a nervous hand to Freya and, after a tense moment of hesitation, Freya took it. Daisy hoped that would be an end to it. At least, now that her friends knew her true identity, she could begin to get on with her life. The only thing that bothered her was that once everyone else in Pencarrow knew the truth about her, she wasn't sure she'd be able to stay.

★ ★ ★

When Lex arrived later that evening, Daisy told him about what had happened and who had been giving her all the grief and trouble.

'Freya? The woman in the glass shop?'

'Uh-huh. Her grandmother lost all her money and killed herself.'

'Yes, I remember that. But even so, to do what she's been doing to you . . . ' He looked furious. His jaw had tightened and his eyes darkened. In fact, he looked dangerous; so dangerous that Daisy was thankful she'd left out the bit about the violence that Freya had subjected her to. Who knew what he'd do if she'd told him? She had a strong suspicion that he would call the police.

'It's understandable in a way,' Daisy said. 'Anyway, she's promised to stop, so hopefully in time we can become friends.'

'Friends? After what she's done?'

'Yes.' She regarded him uneasily. 'Lex,' she began, 'my true identity will soon become public knowledge.'

He eyed her. 'Ye-es.'

'Well, do you want to have your name linked with mine?'

'Why on earth wouldn't I?' He looked genuinely astonished at her question.

'I'm the wife of a fraudster.'

'That's not your fault. That's his fault.' He caught hold of her by the shoulders. 'Look, I love you. I want to spend the rest of my life with you. It'll be a five-minute wonder, and then people will forget.'

'I hope so,' she murmured doubtfully. 'They didn't in Formby.'

'Formby?'

'Yes, that's where I lived, not Liverpool.'

'Any more little secrets to tell me?' he drily asked.

'Sorry, I forgot about that. But I was

pointed at and talked about for weeks and weeks. Like here, my windows were smashed, and my door daubed with obscenities.'

'Oh, my love.' The warmth of his gaze enfolded her along with his arms. 'I'm sure that won't happen here. Cornish folk are very nice people. Once they know the truth, they'll not blame you. And when we've caught up with Grant and he's brought back to face justice, everyone will be much happier. They may even get some of their money back.' He held her away from him then, his expression one of uncertainty. 'There's something I need to tell you, and I don't want you to panic, but my parents want to meet you. I've said we'll go tomorrow morning.'

15

'Oh no,' Daisy moaned. 'What will they say when they know the truth about me? About who I really am? Your father especially. He'll hate me.'

'Calm down. He knows. I've already told him. I've also told him how I feel about you.'

'You have?' Her eyes widened in horror. Oh God. 'Wh-what did he say?'

'I explained what had happened, and he and my mother understand that the fraud had nothing to do with you. Nothing. They're just happy that I'm happy.' He smiled tenderly at her. 'At last.'

'Oh Lex, really?'

'Yes, my darling. Really.'

Despite his words of reassurance, her stomach churned with dread at the thought of the ordeal that might lie ahead of her. Would there be more recriminations? More demands to know why she hadn't realised what Grant was doing? Oh God. She felt sick.

★   ★   ★

But all of Daisy's fears proved groundless. Lex's parents were every bit as charming as she remembered from their visit to his house while she'd been there, and they both looked genuinely delighted to know she and Lex would be getting married.

'Welcome to our family,' his father eventually said.

His mother simply beamed and hugged Daisy tightly. 'I can't begin to imagine what you've been through, my dear,' she said.

Daisy felt the sting of tears in her eyes. 'Oh, thank you; thank you so much.'

Later that afternoon, her parents returned from their trip. Lex had left once they'd been to his parents' house, as he had an appointment he couldn't miss. Eve walked into the kitchen, took one look at the freshly repaired window and asked, 'Have you had a new window fitted?'

'No. Just the pane of glass.'

'Did you break it?' her father put in.

'No, *I* didn't.'

'So who did, if you didn't?' Eve was frowning by this time.

'We-ell, it was broken when I returned from St Austell on Wednesday.' She went on to tell her parents about everything that had been happening to her.

'Oh no,' Eve cried, 'not here as well.'

'Don't worry, Mum. I know who's been behind it.'

'You do?'

'Yes. It's Freya. She recognised me right from the start. She'd seen the newspaper photos of me — kept the cuttings, in fact. Her gran lost all her money to Grant's scheme and-and then she killed herself. She leapt from the headland just above here.'

'Oh my God! Do you mean the woman in the glass shop?' Daisy nodded. 'Well, I can understand her grief, but really — you considered her a friend,' she indignantly said. 'And to do what she's been doing . . . well. Why didn't she say something to you? Say she knew, instead of tormenting you in such a cruel fashion? Mind you, I did think there was something weird about her. I didn't take to her at all. She was very snide to you. Have you reported it to the police?'

'No. She's promised to stop.'

'I don't understand. How did she know? You look quite different now from the newspaper photographs, what with your hair colour and new style. Plus, you've lost weight.'

'Well, obviously I don't look different enough,' Daisy retorted. 'A couple of people thought they knew me when I first arrived, but they didn't realise how. Anyway, all my friends know now. Freya told them all at the rehearsal last night.'

Eve was horrified and didn't try to hide it. 'How did they react?'

'They were wonderful. They all believed me when I told them I'd known nothing about it.'

'Oh, Daisy, darling.'

'Come here, love,' Tom said, opening his arms to her.

Daisy walked straight into them. 'Oh, Dad, it's been truly dreadful.' Her voice broke as the tears began.

'You should have told us,' Eve said. 'We'd have come straight away.'

'I-I didn't want to worry you both.'

'Oh, love.' Her father dropped a kiss onto the top of her head.

It was at that precise moment that the sound of the front door opening reached the three people in the kitchen. Lex called, 'Daisy?'

'In here,' she replied, swiftly wiping any evidence of the tears she'd shed from her face as she pulled back from her father's embrace.

'Who's that?' her mother asked.

Before Daisy could say anything, Lex strode into the kitchen, his gaze swiftly taking in the tableau before him.

'Lex,' Daisy began, 'I was just telling Mum and Dad about Freya.' *This could be a bit awkward*, she mused. She'd hoped to have the time to explain

Lex's present role in her life before he actually turned up. *Oh well, here goes,* she thought. *Get it over with.* Even so, her voice quivered as she said, 'Mum and Dad, meet Lex Harper.'

'Oh,' was all Eve said, as she held out her one hand towards him. 'So nice to meet you, Mr Harper.' She then swivelled her somewhat startled gaze back to Daisy and mouthed, 'He has a key?'

Daisy ignored that. 'I told you about Lex, Mum,' she went on. 'I did some work for him.'

'Yes, I remember,' Eve said. 'But I thought you'd finished with that.'

'I did, but Lex and I . . . He knows everything by the way — who I am and what Grant did.' Should she tell her parents about her and Lex's plan to marry? Or did Lex want to keep it a secret for now, even though his own parents knew?

However, Lex being Lex, he took matters into his own hands and said, 'I'm so glad you're here. I have to tell you, I want to marry Daisy — if that's okay with you both. She has agreed.'

Daisy stared at him, totally bemused by this. He was actually asking her parents for their consent. However, she swiftly realised it had been exactly the right thing to do, because her father immediately stepped forward, his face wreathed in a smile as, following his wife's lead, he held out his hand. 'If that's what Daisy wants, then it's fine by us. Isn't it, love?' he asked his wife, bestowing a meaningful glance upon her; a glance that said, 'Don't argue.'

'Oh, well — yes. Daisy?' Eve glanced at her daughter. 'Are you sure you're okay with this?'

'Oh, yes, Mum. Totally.'

'But what about Grant? You're still married to him, aren't you?' Belatedly, Eve didn't look at all sure about the situation.

'That's all in hand, Mrs — ?' Lex raised an enquiring eyebrow at Daisy.

'Lewis, same as mine,' Daisy told him. 'I've reverted to my maiden name.'

'All in hand?' Eve said. 'What do you mean? Have you heard from Grant, Daisy?'

'No, she hasn't,' Lex said. 'I've hired a private detective to find him. I've used him before and he's never let me down.'

Eve stared at him, visibly lost for words. Daisy couldn't actually remember that ever happening before. Her mother always had something to say about every situation.

'Are you quite, quite sure about this?' Eve again asked her daughter. She was beginning to eye Lex with more than a little suspicion. It was the casual mention of a private detective that had worried her, Daisy guessed.

'Yes, Mum. We love each other, and as soon as I'm able to divorce Grant, we're getting married.'

And that was that.

* * *

Much later, Lex had returned to his own home and Daisy and her parents were in the sitting room along with Ollie, discussing all that had happened. Eve, in particular, looked agitated and anxious.

'Are you sure about marrying him, darling? Does he have a history? I have to say, he seems very nice; but then again, you haven't known him long. And he clearly moves in a very different world to you, what with employing private detectives.' She sniffed her disapproval.

'I've known him long enough to be sure I love him, Mum, very much. And yes, he has a history, but at the age of thirty-five one would expect him to. He's divorced and has two daughters, which I believe I've already mentioned.' In truth, she wasn't sure that she had, or at least not in any detail. 'Chloe and Imogen. Chloe . . . ' She paused, not sure quite how to describe the girl. She didn't want to be too critical, and perhaps influence her mother permanently against her. That could cause problems for the future.

'Well, go on,' Eve impatiently urged her. 'Chloe?'

'Well, Chloe might be a bit of a problem. She hopes her parents will get back together. I think Leah might have mentioned her.' In fact, now that she cast her mind back, Leah did mention Chloe when the three of them were in the gallery.

'Oh, yes, I remember now. And is there any chance of that happening?'

'None at all. She's remarried. But there's something else.'

'What?' It was her father speaking this time.

'Lex's father lost a lot of money to Grant.'

'Oh good Lord.' Eve sighed. 'What's he going to say about you and Lex then?'

'He already knows. I've met his parents — this morning, as a matter of fact. They're fine about it. They accept I had nothing to do with it, and they just want Lex to be happy.'

'So it's just Chloe that's the problem, then?' Eve said.

Daisy surreptitiously crossed her fingers. 'I'm sure that will resolve itself in time.'

'Well, let's hope you're right,' Eve tartly

replied. 'Because if it doesn't . . . How old is she?'

'Twelve.'

'Well, a twelve-year-old girl can create a multitude of problems. I remember you at twelve. You could be a right little madam.'

'Yes, okay, Mum. Lex will sort it out, I'm sure.'

But knowing Chloe as she'd come to, Daisy was nowhere near as confident of that as she sounded.

* * *

One thing at least did work out. Lex's private detective traced Grant to Buenos Aires. He'd left a relatively clear trail behind him. In fact, it was a wonder the police hadn't found him weeks ago. Or maybe they had, but hadn't been able to get him back to the UK. They couldn't have informed Daisy of that because her whereabouts weren't known — though surely they would have contacted her parents to find out.

However, by the time Grant's where-abouts were discovered, he was dead. He'd been the victim of a drive-by shooting by some local mobsters whom it was rumoured he'd also defrauded out of a considerable amount of money. Apart from that, he'd also got himself involved in some sort of drugs ring. All in all, it was a miracle he'd survived as long as he had, the detective told Lex.

When Lex told Daisy, despite the fact that Grant had been her husband, all she felt was an enormous sense of relief. She'd been dreading Grant being returned to the UK and everything being dragged through the courts. It would have been on every front page in the country yet again, and Daisy would in all likelihood have found herself once more in the limelight, which was the last thing she wanted. There wasn't even any of the money he'd stolen left, or at least no one could find any, so his vic-tims couldn't be repaid. Daisy did feel bad about that, but there was nothing she could do to put things right.

'So,' Lex said as he pulled her into his arms, 'now all that's cleared up, let's set a wedding date. There's nothing to stop us — not even my dictatorial eldest daughter.'

Daisy laughed. Everything had turned out as she'd hoped. Even Chloe was gradually starting to come round, and seemed to have accepted her as her father's soon-to-be wife. This was mainly due to the persuasions of her grandparents, Daisy suspected, though she too had talked to Chloe and told her how deeply she loved Lex. Chloe had grudgingly accepted this, much to Daisy's relief. In fact, she and Imogen had readily agreed to be bridesmaids, and that was the proverbial icing on the cake for Daisy.

She asked Lex now, 'How do you feel about a New Year's wedding?'

'Fantastic,' he said.

Eve and Tom had left Blue Haven a couple of days before, and returned home in the sure knowledge that their daughter's situation had been resolved. Daisy had sighed happily as she'd waved them off. Finally her troubles were at an end, and she and Lex were all set to marry. Both sets of parents were pleased about this, thankfully.

Now that she was alone once more, Lex was spending almost every night with her, only returning to his own home on the evenings that Chloe and Imogen were there. Daisy had never realised how truly wonderful real love could be. It made her understand that she'd never loved Grant, not in the way she loved Lex.

She looked down now at her pet and said, 'How about a walk before Lex gets here?' It was only three o'clock, so it wasn't too dark to go. The day had been a bright one, cold but sunny, so it meant daylight for a little bit longer. 'Cliff top?' she asked. 'If we're quick.' Ollie barked enthusiastically.

They set off, not noticing the figure standing motionless at the top of the hill that led ultimately into the town.

It only took ten minutes for Daisy and Ollie to reach the cliff top, where instead of perching on the wooden bench they carried on walking along the narrow pathway. Daisy had let Ollie off the lead; he knew he had to stay close to her. The path wasn't the one they normally took; this one skirted the ruined castle on the sea side.

Belatedly, she was uneasy about the huge drop to the left of them. 'Stay close, Ollie,' she cautioned. 'Maybe I should put your lead back on.'

She'd bent down to do just that when a woman's voice hailed her. 'Daisy, hold up.'

Daisy swung around. Freya was striding towards her. 'Freya,' she said, 'shouldn't you still be at the shop?' Other than at the rehearsals, she'd barely seen the other woman since their fight. Daisy had kept her distance, as had Freya, so she was surprised to see her now.

'I closed for the afternoon; there were no customers about. So I decided to have a walk.'

'Oh. How are you?' Daisy made her tone as friendly as she could, which was quite difficult because she couldn't rid herself of her sense of misgiving, of nervousness, about Freya.

That feeling was intensified tenfold when Freya didn't answer her question. Instead she said, 'I thought it was about time we had a real talk. So when I saw you coming up here, I decided . . . ' She glanced around. 'Well, it's the perfect place, isn't it? No one to disturb us.'

Daisy swallowed. What was Freya doing all the way out here? She recalled all the other times the woman must have watched her from the shadows. Had Freya been watching her today from somewhere? It seemed likely. She didn't believe for a moment that this encounter was down to chance. She'd followed Daisy.

'I thought we'd said all we had to,' Daisy said.

'Not by a long chalk. I heard about your and Lex's engagement.'

'Did you? Well, it's not a secret.' Daisy shrugged, struggling to suppress her growing feeling of fear.

'I'm not letting you have him, you know.'

'Y-you aren't?'

'No. So I decided to come and-and . . . '

'And?' Daisy glanced around. The light was starting to fade. It would soon be dark. She looked down at Ollie. He was sitting, watching her and Freya, his head cocked to one side.

'To tell you to end your engagement. He's mine. He was always meant to be mine. If you hadn't come along, he would have been. You've had my money.'

'Your gran's money, don't you mean?' Daisy quietly asked.

'It would have been mine, eventually. You're not having that and Lex. I won't let you.'

Freya had moved closer. Her eyes were blazing with a febrile light. Her face was flushed. Daisy could feel her hot breath on the skin of her own face. Ollie, getting to his feet, began to growl deep in his throat; clearly he too was sensing the air of menace emanating from Freya.

'Shut up.' Freya aimed a kick at him. Ollie didn't hesitate; he clamped his jaws around her ankle. Freya lashed out again, with even more vigour. Ollie yelped and let go of her.

'Control your bloody dog or he goes over the edge. And don't think I don't mean it, because I don't make empty threats.'

Daisy looked down at Ollie and murmured, 'Ollie, it's okay. Sit.'

They were only a couple of feet away from the cliff edge, three at the most. Daisy could hear the waves thundering against the rocks below. The rocks that, if Ollie went over, would prove lethal. She began to inch away from the cliff edge towards what she hoped would be safety. Ollie followed suit.

'Freya, please — what is it you want? If it's the money back, I'll see what I can do; borrow it, maybe. But please don't hurt Ollie.'

'Oh,' Freya snorted, 'it's not Ollie I intend to hurt.'

'Then what?' A sensation of terror

was building in Daisy as it slowly dawned on her exactly what it was that Freya intended. She intended to hurt her, if that was the only way she could have Lex. Freya was insane, that was becoming clearer with every second that passed.

All of a sudden Freya lunged at Daisy, grabbing her by the shoulders and pushing her backwards towards the edge of the cliff top. Daisy tried to push her hands away, but despite her slim build Freya was strong. Too strong. She was also taller than Daisy by three or four inches. Daisy glanced behind and down. Her stomach heaved with terror. The waves were surging over the rocks, one moment engulfing them completely, the next dragging back to reveal their lethally jagged tops. If she went over, she'd have no chance of surviving.

'Freya, what are you doing?' Daisy tried desperately hard to sound calm, but she could hear the panic in her words, so Freya surely would.

'Getting rid of you, that's what I'm

doing!' Freya yelled. 'It's called poetic justice. Because of you, my grandmother killed herself right here, at this very spot. The same thing's going to happen to you.'

'You're mad!'

Ollie was barking frantically now, leaping up and down and making frantic grabs at Freya's legs. Freya kicked him to one side again. Ollie again yelped in pain.

'Getting rid of me won't give you Lex,' Daisy gasped. 'And it won't bring your grandmother back. Would she really want you to do this?'

'Yes, she would. And we'll see whether getting rid of you gives me Lex, won't we?'

Daisy began to scream then, flailing her arms around as she struggled desperately to free herself from Freya's grip. Freya kept pushing her backwards. The drop yawned terrifyingly behind her.

'Freya — please,' she sobbed. 'Ollie — help me!' Her feet slipped backwards. Desperately she searched for some sort of purchase, but she could find nothing. She was on the very edge of the cliff top, one foot suspended over the void. A stone was dislodged and dropped over, then another and another. She heard the splashes far below as they hit the water. She was going, slipping backwards.

'Freya,' she screamed, 'we're going to fall!'

'No, *you're* going to.' She pushed again, hard. Daisy felt herself slipping even further. It was hopeless. She was going to fall and die on the treacherous rocks below. She screamed yet again. Ollie frantically barked, but was clever enough to know that if he leapt at Freya, it could be enough to push both women over the edge to an almost certain death.

Then, just as Daisy felt herself begin to tumble backwards, a hand was reaching for her and yanking her forward to safety, at the same time knocking Freya sideways. Freya released Daisy and fell back onto the ground, to lie there gasping and shouting as she tried to get back up. It was all over in a couple of seconds.

'Ollie,' someone's voice rasped, 'hold her down.'

The dog did so, grabbing hold of Freya's arm with his teeth and placing his two front paws on her chest. He stood over her then, straddling her body, preventing her from getting up.

Sobbing, Daisy looked up at her saviour. Lex enfolded her in his arms, holding her tightly until her sobs eased.

'Daisy, my darling. Thank God I came back early and saw what was happening up here. That crazy woman was trying to push you over.' His voice shook and he held her even tighter against him. 'Christ, I've never moved so fast in my life. And when I heard you screaming, but couldn't see you — and I could hear Ollie barking . . . ' His voice broke. 'I didn't think I was going to make it in time.' His chest was heaving as he fought for control. He must have run all the way up from the cottage.

Daisy stared up at him as he sobbed

for breath. His face was streaked with moisture, and it wasn't only the result of sweating, she realised. He'd really thought he'd be too late to save her. She lifted a hand and tenderly wiped away the wetness. He turned his head and kissed the palm of her hand, panting, 'God, I love you.'

He then took one arm away from her and pulled his mobile from his coat pocket. He pressed in the numbers nine-nine-nine, and with a voice that still shook said, 'Police? I'm on the cliff top at Pencarrow, above Sandy Cove. There's been an attempted murder.'

The police arrived with admirable speed. Apparently they'd been patrolling nearby. Ollie was still standing guard over Freya, who was lying flat on the ground with her eyes tightly closed. Once Daisy, and then Lex, related what had happened, one of the two constables handcuffed Freya, yanked her roughly to her feet, and led her away.

* * *

That evening, Lex made love to Daisy with so much tenderness and love that she found herself crying once again. The deep sobs shook her as she realised she might not have been here to experience this.

Lex held her even closer and murmured, 'Ssh, my love, it's over. She'll be committed once she's had a psychiatric assessment, I shouldn't wonder.' His tone hardened. 'But in any case, you're not staying here alone any longer; you're moving into the hall with me. We'll soon be married, and I want you whole and in one piece for that.'

'Oh Lex,' Daisy sighed, still tearfully, 'I do love you.'

'I know you do,' he confidently agreed.

She gently tapped his arm. 'Don't be so arrogant. I could still cancel things, you know.'

'Try it,' he huskily whispered. 'You'll pretty quickly discover exactly what I'm capable of.'

'Oh, I already know that,' she murmured, slanting a sensuous and gleaming gaze up at him.

'Hussy,' he said, grinning. 'Now be quiet and kiss me, to confirm I was right in my arrogance; to tell me you really do love me. As much as I love you,' he quietly added.

She didn't argue. Ollie, who'd been watching them closely, leapt up onto the settee with them and gave a contented whine as he settled down alongside Daisy.

'He approves, you see,' she said, tenderly stroking her pet's head.

'I should jolly well think so, seeing as I've just saved both his and your lives. Do you think he'll like living at the hall?'

'He'll be happy wherever I am.'

Lex grinned at her. 'That makes two of us then.' He lowered his head to kiss her passionately, and for a very long time.

We do hope that you have enjoyed reading this large print book.

Did you know that all of our titles are available for purchase?

We publish a wide range of high quality large print books including:
Romances, Mysteries, Classics
General Fiction
Non Fiction and Westerns

Special interest titles available in large print are:
The Little Oxford Dictionary
Music Book, Song Book
Hymn Book, Service Book

Also available from us courtesy of Oxford University Press:
Young Readers' Dictionary
(large print edition)
Young Readers' Thesaurus
(large print edition)

For further information or a free brochure, please contact us at:
Ulverscroft Large Print Books Ltd.,
The Green, Bradgate Road, Anstey,
Leicester, LE7 7FU, England.
Tel: (00 44) 0116 236 4325
Fax: (00 44) 0116 234 0205

Other titles in the
Linford Romance Library:

RETURN TO RIVER SPRINGS

Charlotte McFall

Nine years ago Georgia left River Springs, vowing never to return. But now she's back to start a new job — only to discover that the secrets of her past will not stay buried. Before she has a chance to reconcile with her old flame, Detective Justin Rose, an accident lands her daughter in hospital; and when morning comes, the little girl is nowhere to be found. With her life falling apart around her, and Justin demanding answers she doesn't want to give, Georgia begins the desperate search for her daughter . . .

ENDLESS LOVE

Angela Britnell

Twenty years ago Gemma Sommerby and Jack Watson shared a summer romance, but after he left Cornwall she never heard from him again. And now, large as life and twice as handsome, he's back . . . Gemma can't afford to open her heart to him and risk being hurt again — and Jack is just as disconcerted to find she affects him as much as ever. Why did it really go wrong between them all those years ago? And could they still have a future together?

THE EMERALD

Fay Cunningham

Cassandra Moon knows her mother Dora has a special talent — but will it be enough to protect the eccentric older lady when she is abducted in the depths of winter? Once again, Cass finds herself teaming up with DI Noel Raven, whom she argues with and is attracted to in equal measures. But the only way she and Noel can save Dora is to accept the bond of love that joins them together, so they can harness the power of the emerald ring and bring down the evil Constantine . . .

TROPICAL MADNESS

Nora Fountain

Paediatrician Serena Blake's idea of adventure is applying for a new hospital job in Dorset. Then her brother introduces her to the ruggedly handsome journalist and adventurer Jake Andrews, and she finds herself agreeing to accompany him to the African jungle in order to help sick and injured children. Soon the pair find themselves in the middle of an impending coup. And to make matters worse, Serena discovers that she's falling in love with Jake, though she's sure he will forget about her once — and *if* — they get back home . . .